MURDER IN A COASTAL TOWN
and other stories

By Eric Lee

I0547490

Paragon Publishing
Professional Fiction Publisher
El Sobrante, California, USA

Author website: www.ericleestories.com

For information address:

 Paragon Publishing
Professional Fiction Publisher
2300 Greenridge Drive
El Sobrante, California, 90274

Author website: www.ericleestories.com

Substantial discounts on bulk quantities of this author's publications are available to corporations, educational disciplines, professional associations, and other qualified organizations. For details and specific discount information, visit ericleestories.com and click on the "Contact Us" link at the bottom of the website. For more information about the author's stories, visit ericleestories.com

Printed in the United States of America

Murder in a Coastal Town and other stories
    Eric Lee
    Library of Congress Catalog Number: 2006909893 (first printing)
    ISBN: 0-9674476-2-3

Table of Contents

Dedication

For all of my family and friends
who have supported my writing

Special thanks to the following people who have helped me greatly in my writing:

Alexandria Chun
John Cmelak
Ellen Hanscom
Gary Kurtzman
Brian Lee
Clarence Lee
Gloria Lee
Damon Maxey
Jaelynn Mayes
Bill Raynolds
Mike Sutton
Patrick Sutton
Michael Wiley

Murder in a Coastal Town

I stood in the hallway, looking into Tyler's room. It hadn't changed a bit over the last month: the same posters on the wall, the pillows arranged on the bed in the exact same pattern, his board games neatly stacked in the corner. I've had a hole in my heart, ever since someone murdered my eight-year-old son. Words cannot describe how much I miss him. I have been a detective in the homicide division for fifteen years, so feelings of anger joined my deep sorrow since I had yet to bring Tyler's murderer to justice.

"Dad," a voice said, followed by a tug on my arm. It was my eleven-year-old daughter, Ashley. "I finished talking to Uncle Roger. Can we go for ice cream now?"

I closed Tyler's door and turned toward Ashley. "Yes, of course honey," I said, forcing myself to smile. "Put your shoes on and sit in the car. I'll see if Uncle Roger would like to join us."

Roger was my older brother, who was visiting from out of town. It was good to have him around because he was family, and the fact that he was a child psychologist made it even better. He was here to help Ashley deal with the trauma of having seen her brother murdered. I also hoped he could uncover something she would remember that would provide a lead in the investigation.

Eric J. Lee

I walked down the hallway and into the study, closing the door behind me. Roger was sitting in the large leather chair behind the desk. "Well, how did it go?"

"Have a seat," Roger said, gesturing toward a nearby chair. I sighed before taking a seat. "Before we talk about Ashley, how are you doing?"

"I'm fine."

"You're not fine. You can't possibly be fine. A year ago, you find out your son has cancer. You go to specialist after specialist, giving him the best treatment money can buy. You go into debt, so much so that a month ago, you ask me for a loan. Then, your son is murdered and you spend the last thirty days trying to find the assailant. So... how on earth can you be fine?"

I looked at Roger for a moment. "What do you want from me?"

"I want you to admit your physical and emotional limits. I want you to stop investigating Tyler's death. Leave that to other guys in the department. Psychologically, you could really benefit by taking a break from this."

"I'll take a break when Tyler's murderer is rotting in jail. Now, I would like to hear..." I stopped in mid-sentence as I spotted the picture of Tyler and me on the wall. We both had big grins on our faces during a recent fishing trip. An overwhelming sense of sadness came over me. I buried my face in my hands. "Why? Why would anyone want to kill Tyler? It doesn't make any sense."

"You're right, it doesn't," Roger said, rubbing my shoulder. He had gotten up from his chair and was now standing over me. "I know it's very little consolation, but if Tyler were alive, he would likely be in pain now and would probably only have weeks to live."

"We don't know that. The doctors could have been wrong. There was always hope."

8

Roger stopped rubbing my shoulder. "You took him to five different specialists. They all said that his condition was terminal, giving him two months to live."

"It doesn't matter. Whatever time Tyler had left was his," I said, looking directly at Roger. "Please, tell me how your conversation with Ashley went."

"It went okay. The good news is that, under the circumstances, she's coping well. But, she's feeling neglected. You have been so consumed with finding Tyler's killer, you haven't spent much time with her."

"I'm going to take her out for some ice cream as soon as we finish talking." I scratched my head. "Did she talk about what she witnessed at the cliff?"

"Yes, but it was the same story she has always said."

"Well, tell me again."

"She said she and Tyler took a walk along the cliffs near the lighthouse. She was holding Tyler's hand, when all of a sudden, someone came from behind them, shoved her to the side, and pushed Tyler off the cliff."

"Did she say whether she remembered anything about this person?"

"Just that he wore a hooded sweatshirt," Roger said. "And the hood was over his head."

In the last month, I had made no headway in finding this hooded man. As a detective, my expertise was piecing together evidence, but in this case, there simply was not much of it. I was also good at extracting evidence by interrogating suspects. I made them see that they were better off talking. My motto: Keeping a potential case out of the courtroom is the best way to ensure justice. Unfortunately, I didn't have any suspects. All I had was one witness.

"Maybe, I should talk to her," I said.

"I wouldn't advise that," Roger said, shaking his head. "She's in a fragile stage right now."

"I understand, but with each day that passes, we become less likely to ever catch the creep who did this. I have to talk to her." I looked at my watch, knowing my wife, Christine, would be home soon. "You stay here. Tell Christine that Ashley and I went out for some ice cream."

I drove to the ice cream shop down the street. Ashley got her favorite: a chocolate ice cream cone with sprinkles. We walked to the car as she continued to enjoy her cone. Absorbed in telling a story about her best friend, Ashley didn't notice that I'd driven to the path that led up to the cliffs.

I got out of the car and walked around to open Ashley's door. When I opened the door, she did not want to get out. "What are we doing here?" Her expression had changed from happy to frightened.

"Oh honey," I said, crouching down in a catcher's position. "Everything is okay." I reached out my hand. She timidly reached out her hand to touch mine. I helped her out of the car, and closed the door. "Come on, let's go for a walk."

Ashley jerked back a bit. She pointed at the cliff. "That's where Tyler fell. I don't want to go back there."

"I know you're a little scared. I am too, but I need you to be a big girl. There's a memorial set up for Tyler, with nice cards and beautiful flowers. Now, it will be just a few minutes and it would really mean a lot if you came with me. Can you do that for me?"

Ashley nodded and we slowly made our way along the dirt path toward the cliff. As we got closer, Ashley gripped my hand tighter. The sun peeked in between the patches of dark clouds above. To our right was a steep cliff with waves crashing against the rocks below. I bit my lower lip as I wrestled with what I was about to do. We had reached Tyler's memorial, decorated with flowers, pictures, and a large cross. Ashley looked at it, speechless.

"Ashley," I said, kneeling down in front of her. "I need you to close your eyes for me." Ashley's forehead wrinkled, not clear of the purpose for my request. "Please, honey." Ashley closed her eyes, as she held the melting ice cream cone in her right hand. "Just relax and listen to the waves. Smell the fresh air and try to remember the day you and Tyler came up here."

Ashley opened her eyes. "I don't want to think about that."

"Ashley, honey, you have to keep your eyes closed. I'm right here. Everything is going to be okay." Ashley closed her eyes again. "Feel the dirt path with your feet. Tell me about your walk with Tyler that morning," I said, in as soothing a tone as I could muster.

"Tyler wanted to go up to the lighthouse to watch the sailboats. He held my hand as we walked up there. And then…" Ashley stopped abruptly, dropping her ice cream cone on the ground. She opened her eyes, looking terrified.

"You're okay, honey. What happened next?"

"Tyler fell," Ashley said, beginning to sob.

"How did he fall?"

"Someone pushed him."

"Who, who pushed him?" I asked, grabbing hold of Ashley by her arms. When she didn't answer immediately, I asked again, inadvertently tightening my grip.

"A man… a man in a hooded sweatshirt," Ashley said, with tears flowing down her face. "I don't want to talk about it."

"I understand," I said before hugging her. I held her tightly and whispered in her ear, "It's okay, dad's here. I just need you to describe this man." Just then, my cell phone rang. I let go of Ashley and reached into my pocket to look at the phone. The call was coming from my house. "Hello."

"Hi, it's me," the voice said. It was my wife, Christine. "Are you with Ashley?"

"Yeah, she's right here."

"Dad, I want to go home," Ashley said between sniffles.

"That's Ashley. Is she crying? Where did you take her?"

"Everything is okay," I said. "We'll be home in a few minutes."

"I can hear waves crashing in the background," Christine said. "You took her to the cliffs. How could you!"

"Relax Christine. Everything is fine."

"You bring her home right now."

"Okay, okay," I said before hanging up.

I put the phone back in my pocket, and spent the next few minutes trying to calm Ashley down. Then, I said to her, "We're going home, but I just need you to close your eyes for another moment and relax." I wiped a lone tear off her face and brushed her hair back, tucking it behind her ears. "You know your dad loves you, right?" Ashley nodded and I kissed her on the cheek. "Now, what happened after the man shoved you?"

Ashley paused a moment as she tried to gather her thoughts. "He shoved me onto the ground. And then, I saw him push Tyler off the cliff." Ashley paused to swallow hard. "I was on the ground. I was scared. I thought he would do the same to me. I looked up at him and he looked down at me."

"So, you saw his face? This is important, honey. What did he look like?"

Just then, a car came to a halt on the street in the distance. I recognized the car. Christine and Roger jumped out of the car. I focused back on Ashley, knowing I was running out of time. "Describe the man in the hooded sweatshirt."

Ashley turned around and exclaimed, "Mom!"

I shook her slightly. "Ashley, look at me and think hard. Was the man who pushed Tyler old or young? Fat or skinny? Describe him."

Finally, Ashley blurted out, "It was you. He looked exactly like you!" I reflexively let go of her as I had trouble believing my ears.

"What do you mean it was me?" I asked. "I'm here now. Who did you see in the hooded sweatshirt? Who pushed Tyler off the cliff?"

"I told you. It was you, dad! You did it."

My jaw dropped. I couldn't believe what I was hearing. Within the next couple of seconds, Christine arrived and embraced a sobbing Ashley. "I can't believe you did this. How could you take our daughter here? Look what you've done to her."

"I was trying to find out what happened," I said, still on my knees.

"I may never be able to forgive you for this," Christine said, grabbing our daughter's hand and walking her back toward the car. I couldn't move, feeling paralyzed with frustration and regret. I had traumatized my daughter and infuriated my wife. After watching them drive away, I looked at the memorial for Tyler and realized I was still no closer to finding who murdered him.

I collapsed on the dirt path and began sobbing. I had so much pent-up rage about the murder of my child, I hadn't taken time to grieve. Roger sat down next to me, and put his hand on my shoulder. I hadn't cried more than a handful of times in my life. Feeling awkward about my show of raw emotion, I tried to gather myself. I took a couple of slow, deep breaths. "When Christine came home, you told her what I was doing with Ashley, didn't you?" I asked, looking out to sea. I wiped off a remnant of a tear as I focused on a passing ship. "That's why she called me."

"Yes, I did," Roger said. "I was worried about Ashley. You shouldn't have tried to force a conversation with her and you certainly shouldn't have brought her back here."

13

I shook my head. "You don't have a right to say that. Your son wasn't murdered. You haven't watched a month go by and have absolutely no lead to the killer. And with each day that passes, the chances of solving the case go down."

"You had two children. One is dead. There is nothing you can do now to change that. You have to start nurturing and caring for the child who's still alive."

"What do you mean *start*? I have always cared for Ashley."

"Let's be honest," Roger said. "With all of Tyler's medical problems this last year, you have really been far more focused on him. And you certainly haven't cared for her in the last month."

"How can you say that?" I asked, wounded by his words.

"You have put finding Tyler's murderer ahead of everything else, including the welfare of your daughter. I mean, you had to know that bringing her back here would cause pain."

"It's been thirty days since Tyler's death and I haven't pressed her," I said in my defense. "She hadn't been able to recall anything. I had to see, if being back in the environment could trigger her memory."

"Well, it was a bad call." A few moments of silence passed before he asked, "Did you learn anything new?"

A chill went up my spine as I refocused on the fact that Ashley had said that I had killed Tyler. I took a deep breath and exhaled slowly, stalling for time to decide what I would tell Roger. "As a matter of fact, I did. I had her close her eyes and think back to the events of the day. And when we got to the hooded man, she told me who he was."

"Really. Who?"

"Me." There was silence for a few seconds as Roger looked at me in disbelief. "She said I shoved Tyler off the cliff. So tell me doc. What does that mean?"

"Well, it means one of two things. Either she just said that to make you stop pressuring her, or…"

"Or what?"

"She's engaging in association," Roger said. I flashed him a perplexed look. "All that means is that she was so bothered by your interrogation that she sees you as the personification of evil. So evil, in fact, she placed your face on the most hated man in her world, the guy who murdered Tyler." Roger tilted his head as he looked at me, "Either way, you have to stop this. Anyone in the department can find Tyler's killer, but only you can be Ashley's father. She needs her father."

"Alright," I said, standing up. I dusted the dirt from the path off my backside and legs and Roger did the same. "Before we go, I just want to re-enact what happened that day." Roger rolled his eyes. "Please," I said.

"Okay, but this is the last time we do this. Agreed?"

"Yes, yes, last time," I said, waving my hand in the air. "Take me through what happened based on your conversations with Ashley, step by step."

Roger rubbed his chin for a moment as he pondered where to start. "Ashley was walking up with Tyler toward that lighthouse."

"Let's act it out," I said. "You be Ashley and I'll be Tyler." Roger shot me a puzzled look, but agreed to play along. "She was holding Tyler's left hand, so you would be on that side, closest to the cliff." I walked over to Roger's right side and grabbed his hand. Roger began walking in place as he said, "Okay, we're walking, when all of a sudden someone comes up from behind us. He shoves Ashley to the side and then shoves Tyler off the cliff." Roger let go of my hand and staggered a few feet away from me.

"Hold it," I said. "You just said the murderer knocked her to the side, but Ashley told me today that he knocked her to the ground."

"Knocked her to the side, knocked her to the ground. What difference does it make?"

Eric J. Lee

"Maybe all the difference in the world. Why the discrepancy?"

"She probably just misspoke to you. She was probably terrified at being back here."

"She didn't misspeak. She said she was knocked to the ground. She said it twice. Then, she said she looked up and saw the hooded man. She wouldn't have talked about *looking up* if she meant to say she was knocked to the side. So, I ask you again. Why the discrepancy?"

"I don't know," Roger said. "But, we aren't going to figure it out by rehashing it. Can we go now?" Roger began dusting the dirt off the back of his pants, which he had failed to get earlier.

As I watched him, it hit me like a ton of bricks. "Oh my God, the dirt. You still have dirt on the back of your pants."

"Yeah, we were sitting on the ground," Roger said, looking at me as if I were crazy.

"I know why *you* have dirt on you. Ashley told me today she was knocked to this very same ground. Yet, her clothes didn't have any dirt on them."

Roger tilted his head slightly as he squinted. "Wait a minute. What are you saying?"

I paused a moment as a huge lump formed in my throat. "I know that she lied about being knocked to the ground. So, why would she lie?" Roger didn't respond and I didn't wait for an answer. "The only reason I can think of is that she can't keep her story straight. She's covering for herself."

"That's insane."

"Is it?" I asked. "Maybe there was no hooded man. Maybe, she was the one who pushed Tyler off that cliff."

"You don't know that," Roger said, pointing at me. "And I don't think it's worth investigating to determine if you're right. Now, can the detective in you let it go?"

"No, I can't," I said, shaking my head. "But it's not because of the detective in me, it's the father. I can't let the slaughter of my son go unpunished."

"You're Ashley's father too. And, the truth is that we don't know what happened here that day. Maybe Ashley had something to do with it. But, maybe not." Roger leaned closer to me. "You will do irreparable harm to her if you pursue this. I beg of you. Let this go."

I squeezed my eyes shut as I wrestled with a series of emotions. Finally, I nodded and said, "Okay, I'll drop it. It's time I started living in the present as opposed to the past." Roger put his arm around me. As we walked away from the cliffs, I was literally and figuratively leaving the details of Tyler's death behind me. All my police instincts told me that Ashley pushed Tyler off that cliff. I could never believe that it was a premeditated act. Maybe it was an accident. Maybe she just wanted to push Tyler away from her and not off the cliff. Still, the thought that my neglect of Ashley might have driven her to do this was painful.

I could have investigated it, but I think I was too afraid of what I would find. I had already lost one child. I couldn't bear to lose another one.

Later that day, I called my boss at the station and announced that I was taking a three-month leave of absence. I spent the next two months repairing my marriage and nurturing my daughter. I had bonded with Ashley more than ever before. One night, as I was tucking her into bed, she said to me, "I miss Tyler. I miss him a lot."

"Me too," I said.

Ashley looked at me and said softly, "Daddy, I didn't mean for it to happen. I'm sorry." My heartbeat quickened, but I chose not to question her further. I knew what she meant. I kissed her good night and said, "Me too."

Eric J. Lee

Murder at Buckley Liquors

"Mister Douglas, did you hear the question?" a strong voice boomed, breaking my trance. My fifty-five year old heart still raced from hearing the words "murder" and "death penalty" in the same sentence. I instinctively shook my head in an attempt to refocus. "I'll repeat the question then," the judge said. "Can you be objective in a murder case where the sentence could result in the death penalty?"

My heart quickened as an image of an electric chair flashed through my mind. "Yes, I can be objective."

The judge looked over to the prosecuting attorney who glanced at his notes. "The people are satisfied with this jury."

The defendant, a man in his early forties, leaned over to whisper to his attorney. After a few moments, the defense attorney said, "The defense is satisfied with this jury."

After we were sworn in, the judge said, "All of you are jurors in the case of the People vs. Paul Sutton." As he talked, he clasped his hands together. He was what you'd expect a judge to look like. His gray hair and reading glasses made him look distinguished. At the same time, the dark robe and stern facial expression made him look intimidating. Even sitting down, I could tell the judge was a big, tall man. He spoke in a thunderous voice that easily filled the packed courtroom. "We will now hear the people's opening statement."

As the prosecutor rose and approached the jury, he looked very serious, as if he were gearing himself for a tough battle. Devoid of facial hair, he had a boyish face and looked to be thirty years old at most. One thing was for sure, getting a case with this much exposure meant he was highly regarded in the D.A.'s office. Dressed in a blue suit and powerful red tie, he was a picture of confidence and control.

"Well, we know why they're all here," the prosecutor said, gesturing over his right shoulder toward the group of reporters and video cameras. "The defendant is married to our state senator. Despite this, the evidence will show Paul Sutton was a desperate man, who was struggling economically."

"The evidence will show that, that man," he said, pointing to the defendant. "Paul Sutton, with malice and forethought, robbed, shot, and murdered Gary Bender, an innocent convenience store clerk. You will see this cold, callous act with your own eyes because it was all caught by the store's security camera. Although the defendant had a mask on when he committed this horrific crime, the evidence will show, beyond a reasonable doubt, the masked man was Paul Sutton. Two witnesses saw Paul Sutton put on that mask in the parking lot and then walk into the liquor store. The same two witnesses heard gunshots and saw Paul Sutton race out of the store. Another witness saw him speed away from the scene."

The prosecutor paused for a moment as he made eye contact with each juror. "The eye witness testimony will be backed by scientific evidence by a videotape and film expert. He will testify that Paul Sutton is the same sex, height, and weight as the masked murderer on the videotape."

I was simply trying to listen to what the lawyer was saying. But, the middle-aged female juror to my right, who was on the end, was taking copious notes. She wore red-rimmed glasses and had short black hair. She had a serious expression. I glanced down at her pad, curious as to what she could be writing. Then, she looked up at me. When our eyes met, she seemed surprised and slightly perturbed that I was looking at her. I quickly looked away and focused my attention back on the prosecutor.

"Now, despite all the evidence that will place Paul Sutton and his car at the liquor store that fateful night, the defense will tell you he was never there." The prosecutor took a few steps forward and rested his hands on the railing of the juror box. "Please, don't buy that." He asked rhetorically, shrugging his shoulders, "And why shouldn't you buy it? You shouldn't buy it because the defense's story about his whereabouts won't make sense." He paused before repeating as he hit the railing, "It won't make sense."

"This court case is going to come down to one thing. Where was Paul Sutton at 11:33 PM on October 15th? You will hear two versions of his whereabouts." The prosecutor held out his left hand and said, "The people's version will be backed by multiple eye-witness testimonies. It will be backed by observations of individuals who have absolutely no reason to lie. It will be backed with scientific evidence." He held out his right hand, but at a much lower level. "The defendant's version is backed by nothing but what his wife says, a career politician who has everything to lose in this case. I will simply ask you twelve people to use your own common sense. I believe if you look to your heart and to your brain, the defense's version," he said, looking at his right hand and dropping it farther, "Simply won't make sense."

As the prosecutor turned around and sat back down, I scribbled some notes down on my pad. The judge looked at the defense attorney, a woman in her mid 50s. "Your honor, the defense would like to reserve our opening statement."

The judge glanced at his watch. "Counselors, we are getting close to the end of the day. I believe it would be best to hold off any testimony until nine o'clock tomorrow." The judge dropped his head as if to ask if there were any complaints. There were none. The judge turned toward the jury. "Ladies and gentlemen, court is now adjourned. Please remember my admonitions to you. You are not allowed to talk about this case to anyone. You are not allowed to do any investigations or read anything about this case in the newspapers or even watch anything about it on television. You are not to make any conclusions until hearing all of the evidence. You're dismissed!"

As the jury members slowly exited the courtroom, I realized that our jury had exactly six men and six women. One of the women had a metal brace down her right leg and walked with the aid of crutches. I caught up to the attractive, young woman as she approached the door that led out the back exit of the courthouse. I skipped ahead of her to open the door.

"Thank you," the woman said with a smile. I followed her out before introducing myself. "I'm Laura," the woman said, stopping to look at me. "You're the private eye, right?"

"Yeah," I said, surprised she had remembered that from the juror selection process. "You have a good memory." I put my finger up to my lips, struggling to think of Laura's profession. Finally, I said with a sigh, "I don't remember what you do."

"I'm a teacher. I would have thought a private eye would remember everything."

"Let me tell you a secret about private eyes," I said, laughing. "We don't remember much unless we write it down."

The next morning, I walked up to the courthouse, a little tired, but on-time. It was Tuesday, January 19th. It took a couple cups of coffee, but I had made it. I walked up to the waiting area in front of the courtroom and sat down next to another member of the jury. He wore jeans and a red striped shirt and suspenders. I would guess that he was in his early forties. He was about six feet tall with a strong build. He appeared to be in deep thought as he stared off in the distance. "Hi," I said.

"Aye," the man responded in a monotone voice.

"I'm Robert," I said, holding out my hand.

"Name's Howard Nash," the man said, shaking my hand with a firm grip. Howard had thick eyebrows and a stern, unchanging facial expression.

"So, you excited about the trial?" I asked, struggling to make conversation.

"Not excited 'bout nothin'. Should be workin'."

"Oh, what do you do?"

"Gardener."

"Oh," I said, trying to think of something to say. I decided to give up the tiring task of conversation with Howard, instead choosing to remain silent.

The bailiff came out to the waiting area to call us into the courtroom. There was a hushed silence as we entered the packed courtroom and took our seats. We were always supposed to take the same seats in the jury. So, I again sat in the second row sandwiched between an elderly gentleman and the note-taking lady. I had to think back to juror selection to remember what her name was. "You're Nancy, right?" I asked her. She answered me with a nod as she opened her note pad. However, my next comment of "Don't use up all your lead in one day" failed to receive any reaction from her at all.

The judge called the court to order and instructed the prosecution to call their first witness.

"The people call Jason Buckley to the stand." A middle-aged man, who was prematurely losing his hair, calmly walked to the stand. He was wearing a loose-fitting, blue suit that could not hide the fact that he was slightly overweight. He was sworn in and he sat down. "Mr. Buckley, what do you do for a living?"

Eric J. Lee

"I own two liquor stores that I help manage."

"Two liquor stores? Would one be called Buckley Liquors on 136 Addison Street?"

"Yes."

The prosecutor asked to introduce a small photograph as People's Exhibit 1. The judge and the defense consented and the prosecutor asked Buckley, as he handed him the picture, if he recognized the person in the photograph.

"Yes, that's Gary Bender," Buckley said with little emotion as he handed back the picture.

"How do you know him?"

"He was my partner in Buckley Liquors. He worked as a manager at the Addison location."

"You said *was*. He no longer manages the store?"

"No, about three months ago, he was shot and killed by a robber."

Silence filled the courtroom as the prosecutor purposely paused. "How do you know this?"

"Saw it with my own eyes. My store is equipped with two security video cameras."

"Could you describe your security system Mr. Buckley?"

"Well, it's not top of the line, you understand, but my stores just aren't that profitable. Couldn't afford a better one."

"Just tell the court about the system," the prosecutor said, trying to steer him back to the point.

"Well, I have two cameras. The first one is right over the checkout stand. The robber destroyed that one completely. But, a hidden camera on the side picked up the robbery and the murder." Buckley paused for a moment. "Ironically, that was the cheaper camera that Gary installed himself. He was a camera buff."

"Mr. Buckley," the prosecutor said, trying to cut off his rambling. "I'd like to show the jury the videotape which picks up the complete robbery." The prosecutor turned to the judge.

"We will have it set up in a minute." The judge nodded as a bailiff wheeled in a VCR.

"This ought to be interesting," the old man next to me whispered.

"I'll say," I said, realizing that I had never introduced myself to the balding man who appeared to be in his seventies. He was short and looked a little frail. But, he seemed to have an inner energy and spryness that I admired. While they set up the VCR, I learned that his name was David.

"Okay," the prosecutor said. "I am introducing this videotape as People's Exhibit 2." He showed it to the defense attorney and had it labeled by the clerk. "This will last only about a minute ladies and gentlemen. So, please watch closely."

The prosecutor pushed play on the video recorder and the inside of a liquor store appeared, showing a middle-aged man working behind the counter. Sitting down on a high stool, the cashier was looking down, reading a magazine. Just then, a man walked up to the counter holding a gun. The gunman was average height and wore a Chicago Bulls jacket. Because the robber was wearing a black mask, it was impossible to identify him.

The cashier jumped up from his chair and raised his hands. I watched closely as the gunman shot holes through the other camera, destroying it. Then, the gunman yelled something. The camera apparently did not pick up sound. The obviously shaken cashier began taking money out of the cash register and dumping it in the gunman's bag. When he finished, the cashier put up his hands back up defensively. The gunman mouthed something before shooting him twice in the heart. I heard a collective gasp in the jury box. I swallowed hard as I stared at the video. The cashier fell to the floor behind the counter. The gunman paused for a second and raced around the counter as if to see if his victim was indeed dead. The counter obstructed the camera view. I'd say he was behind the counter for ten seconds

Eric J. Lee

before the gunman jumped up, grabbed his bag and raced out of the store.

The videotape stopped and the prosecutor turned off the television before walking back to Buckley who was still on the stand. "Is the tape we just viewed in this courtroom the same tape you saw?"

"Yes," Buckley responded.

"We saw numbers at the top right part of the screen. Was that the time?"

"Yes. It was 11:33 PM." I quickly jotted down the time on my notepad.

"Now, what kind of lighting do you have outside your stores at night?"

"Oh they're pretty well lit," Buckley responded as if on cue.

"How about the parking lot?"

"Oh yeah. We've got three large lights in the parking lot."

"Mister Buckley. Is it important for you to keep the parking lots of your stores well lit at night?"

"Absolutely. It's important for business, for two reasons. First of all, it lets people know that we're still open. Don't want to lose business at midnight 'cuz people think the store is closed because the parking lot is dark. And second, it makes customers feel safer. A well lit parking lot makes wary customers more likely to come in at night."

The prosecutor introduced a large diagram as People's Exhibit 3. It showed the position of the phone booth, parking lot, and the entrance to Buckley Liquors. The exhibit showed that Buckley Liquors was located at the corner of Addison Street and Central Road. "Do you know where the phone booth is located at your store on Addison Street?"

"Yes," Buckley said. "It's located at the southwest corner of the parking lot, at the corner of the liquor store building."

Murder at Buckley Liquors

"Now, if you were to stand in the phone booth at night, could you recognize the make and model of a car pulling into the parking lot?"

"Sure could. Like I said, the place is well-lit."

"Well-lit," the prosecutor repeated before smiling. "Thank you, Mr. Buckley. No further questions."

The defense attorney walked up to the stand, with confidence and purpose. "How much money was taken out of the cash register?"

"About one hundred and seven dollars."

"Only one hundred and seven dollars?"

"Yeah," Buckley said uneasily, as he slightly squirmed in his seat. "The robber didn't get the money in the cash register under the tray. All the big bills are kept there."

"Mr. Buckley, there is no doubt that you were robbed, but, the question is, was the defendant the one who committed the crime. Under oath, can you say the defendant robbed you?"

"No."

"And Mr. Buckley, would you tell the court when was the last time you stood in this phone booth at 11:30 at night and identified incoming cars?" Buckley froze for a moment. "Did you hear the question? Shall I repeat it?"

"No, I heard it. I never have."

"Then, how could you say that you could identify the car in the parking lot from the phone booth?"

"Well, you can see the cars from inside the store easily. It's about the same distance. So, I assumed that you could see it from the phone booth."

"You assumed?" the defense attorney said, acting shocked. She shook her head and told the judge that she had no further questions. The prosecution declined to question the witness again and the defense attorney asked Buckley to remain subject to recall.

The judge turned to Buckley. "You're free to go, but you may be called back later to testify again." Buckley nodded and walked out of the courtroom.

The prosecuting attorney stood up. "The people would like to call Ms. Sallie Anderson." A skinny woman in her early thirties walked to the stand. As she clung to her purse, she appeared frightened and looked very pale. She clenched her fist tightly as she was sworn in. As she settled in the witness chair, she appeared frail and vulnerable.

"I'm showing Ms. Anderson People's Exhibit 1," the prosecutor said, handing her the small photograph. "Do you know this person?"

Ms. Anderson closed her eyes for a moment before handing the photo back. The sight of the picture had an obvious effect on her. "Yes, that's my late fiancé, Gary Bender."

"When were you going to be married?"

Ms. Anderson wiped her eyes before she said, "February 24th. About a month from now. He already bought an engagement ring." I looked at the ring as Ms. Anderson held her hand up. I couldn't tell if it was a real diamond. But, it appeared to be solid gold and it was large. "We were going to take a European cruise for our honeymoon."

"It sounds like you two had wonderful plans," the prosecutor said, trying to comfort his witness.

"We were going to buy a house off the beach. We were..."

"Objection, your honor," the defense attorney said, rising. "Relevance?"

"Sustained," the judge said.

The prosecutor did not seem fazed by the judgment. Instead, he turned his attention back on Ms. Anderson. "When did you last see your fiancé, Gary Bender alive?"

"The day he was killed, October 15th." Ms. Andersen clung to her purse in her lap like a security blanket. "That was Friday night. He always worked at the liquor store on Friday nights.

We had an early dinner and he left at about 6:15, so he could get to work to begin his shift at 6:30."

"One more question," the prosecuting attorney said as if to assure Ms. Anderson that it was almost over. "Did you or Gary Bender know the defendant or his wife?"

"Well, I never met either of them, but I believe Gary knew Senator Sutton." The prosecutor said he had no further questions and I looked down on my notepad, unsure what light Ms. Anderson shed on the case.

The defense attorney rose cautiously. "Ms. Anderson. You said that Gary knew Senator Sutton. Did he know the defendant, Paul Sutton?"

"He never said anything about him," Ms. Anderson responded meekly.

"Okay," the defense attorney said, approaching Ms. Anderson. "You said Gary knows Senator Sutton. So, being Gary's fiancée, when was the last time you saw Gary with Senator Sutton?"

"I never have."

"So, when you say Gary knows Senator Sutton, you're not basing that on any firsthand knowledge, just that he said that he knew her?"

"I guess so."

"Well, since Gary supposedly knew Senator Sutton, tell me some things that he said they did."

Ms. Anderson seemed to go blank as she stared off in the distance. "Gary never gave any specifics. He only said that he knew her."

"I guess that it's nice to tell people that you know someone famous," the defense attorney commented before saying that she had no further questions. Like Buckley, the defense wanted Ms. Andersen to be subject to recall.

"The people would like to call Alan Clark to the stand." A boy in his mid-teens and wearing a preppy sweater walked quickly into the courtroom and up to the stand. The boy looked prim and proper, appearing to have a recent haircut. I bet the prosecution spent hours transforming him. As the prosecutor approached the stand, Alan stared directly at him as if he were trying to avoid looking at the defendant, the jury, and the large audience.

"Are you nervous Alan?" the prosecutor asked.

"Little bit," Alan answered, wiping a little sweat from his brow.

"No reason to be. All we want you to do is tell the truth. Do you know Paul Sutton?"

"Yes, I do."

"Is he in the courtroom now?"

"Yes, he is," Alan said, still looking directly at the prosecutor.

"Can you identify him?"

Alan looked away from the prosecutor and pointed at the defendant. "The man behind the table wearing a blue suit and gray tie."

The prosecutor turned and looked at the judge. "Let the record reflect that the witness has identified the defendant." The judge consented and the prosecutor turned back to Alan. "How do you know Mr. Sutton?"

"He was my Algebra II teacher at my high school."

"You took your second year of Algebra in high school. What grade are you in?"

"I'm a junior now," Alan responded. "But, I took the class when I was a sophomore. I'm a year ahead in math."

"So, you observed him every day, Monday through Friday, for an entire school year?"

"Yeah," Alan said, nodding.

"Now, I want you to think back to October 15th. That was a Friday. Can you tell me what happened that night?"

"Yeah, uh, I was at a party at my friend's house."

"What were you doing at this party?"

"Kicking back. We had the music blaring, some dancing, talking." Alan added with a shoulder shrug, "You know, having a good time."

"Were you drinking alcohol?"

"No. I don't drink."

"Were you doing drugs?"

"No, I don't do drugs."

"So how long did you stay at the party?"

"From nine until a little after eleven. Then, we walked to Buckley Liquors to pick up some more stuff for the party. It's only two blocks away."

"We?" the prosecutor asked.

"Me and a buddy of mine, Brad Logan."

"What happened after you arrived at Buckley Liquors?"

"We bought some stuff and left the store, but Brad wanted to call a friend who hadn't come to the party. He wanted to know why she hadn't come. We were going to tell her we could walk over to her house and take her to the party."

"So where did you call her from?"

"There's a public telephone at Buckley Liquors."

At this moment, the prosecutor brought out People's Exhibit 3, the large diagram of Buckley Liquors. "Alan," the prosecutor said, pointing to the diagram. "Is this diagram an accurate picture of Buckley Liquors, including the parking lot and phone booth?"

"Yeah, it's accurate," Alan said. "From the phone booth, I could see the parking lot clearly. Brad was talking on the phone when I noticed a red Porsche 914 pull into the parking lot." Alan went on to say that the car parked in front of the entrance to the store.

"Alan, after the incident, you were able to measure the approximate distance that the phone booth was from the parked car. Isn't that correct?"

"Yes."

"And how far was that?"

"About 25 feet."

"So, at 25 feet, did you recognize the car?"

"Yes," Alan said with a serious look. "It was Mister Sutton's."

"Paul Sutton?"

"Yes."

"How can you be sure?"

"Well, I'm seventeen years old. I'm driving now, you know. And I can't wait 'till I have enough money to buy a car of my own. That's the car I want. I know every inch of that car. I think I've read every brochure and report ever written on that car."

"Okay, you know that a Porsche 914 pulled into Buckley Liquors' parking lot. But, how do you know if it was the defendant's car?"

"Cuz, Mister Sutton drives that car to school most of the time. And I've spent my lunch hour admiring it in the teacher's lot on the other side of the school. It's a perfect car. That is, until someone keyed it."

"Alan, explain to the jury what you mean by keyed."

"Someone took a key and scraped the car just above the..." Alan thought for a moment. "The front right tire. This happened in late September, 'bout three weeks before the robbery."

"The car that pulled into Buckley Liquors on the night of the 15th, did it have the same mark?"

"Yeah, it was the same car," Alan insisted. "Had the same scratch, about two feet long."

"Could you see who was driving the car?"

"Yes," Alan said. "When the car pulled up, it caught my attention because I saw the key mark. I knew it was Mister Sutton's car. And when it came to a stop in front of Buckley Liquors, I clearly saw who was driving the car."

"And who was it?"

"It was Mister Sutton, the defendant." I glanced over to Paul who was calmly and quietly taking notes. "As soon as I realized it was Mister Sutton for sure, I yelled for Brad to duck."

"Why did you do that?"

Alan shrugged. "I was just riding on emotions. Mister Sutton was our teacher and he knew how old we were. And we just had bought some beer. And the cases of beer were right at our feet."

"So, when you told Brad to duck, did he do it immediately?"

"Pretty much. The phone booth is mostly glass. But, I'd guess the bottom three feet or so is lined with concrete. So, Brad ducked in the phone booth. I crawled just a few feet over and stood around the corner of the building."

"How long did you stay there hiding?"

Alan thought for a moment. "Until I heard the car door slam. Couldn't have been more than twenty seconds. Then, I peeked around the corner and saw Mister Sutton walk into the store. He had a mask on at that point."

"Were you wondering why your teacher was wearing a mask in the middle of the night as he entered a liquor store?"

"Yeah," Alan said, nodding for emphasis. "But, I thought he was going to pull some prank. Not rob and shoot the cashier."

"What happened after he entered the store?"

"Well, Brad and I were trying to figure out why our teacher was entering the liquor store with a mask. Then, we heard these shots coming from the store."

"What did you do?"

"We ducked behind the phone booth," Alan said, as if it were obvious. "We were scared."

"Then what happened?"

"Then we heard Mister Sutton run out of the store and get into his car. I looked up and saw him drive off, nearly ran over a lady walking her dog."

"Then what did you do?"

"We called the police. Then we went inside and saw the cashier dead."

The prosecutor slowly walked away from Alan and said, "You're saying you saw a lot. You saw Mr. Sutton's car, the key mark, and Mr. Sutton. Is that right?"

"Yes."

"Alan, a lot of your testimony is based on what you saw. Therefore, I must ask you. How is your vision?"

"It's great. I've been tested both before and after October 15th. I have 20/20 vision."

The prosecutor said that he did not have any further questions. The defendant whispered something to his attorney and the defense attorney looked primed and ready to attack the witness. But, the judge said, "Let's take a recess for lunch. We will reconvene at 1:15." He gave us the quick lecture about not discussing the case and left the bench.

The jury slowly exited the courtroom. As I exited the building, I held the door open for Laura, the juror on crutches. She was accompanied by an elderly woman, who carried a knitting bag. After an introduction, I learned her name was Catherine.

In her late sixties, Catherine had completely gray hair and some wrinkles on her face. She also had a beautiful smile and apparently a pleasant disposition. She said, "We're going to get some sandwiches and sit in the park. Would you like to join us?"

"Sure," I replied.

Just then, a slightly overweight woman, who had just stuck a wad of gum in her mouth, walked over to us. "You all gettin' sandwiches?" Laura nodded her head and asked if she would like to join us. "Count me in," the woman responded, before introducing herself as Barbara.

After picking up our sandwiches, we walked over to the park. If there was one thing I learned on our walk, it was that Barbara loved to talk. "Shall we eat here?" Catherine asked, finding a split second opening to interrupt Barbara's babbling. Everyone agreed and we sat down on a picnic bench.

I began to work on my sandwich when Barbara interrupted her own blabbing to point at a young man walking down the trail and say, "Hey, he's in our jury as well. His name is Jonathan."

As the man approached us, Barbara called out his name and Jonathan seemed to reluctantly walk over to us. He was a skinny, good-looking kid, about average height. He was holding a large stack of flashcards, which he put on the bench as he sat down.

"So, what's with the flashcards?" I asked.

"Going to take the CPA exam," Jonathan replied. "That's a lot of memorization. Flash cards help."

"I think we'll need flashcards for this case," Catherine said.

"The way I figure it," Barbara said, talking with her mouth full of food. "This one's a no-brainer."

"How do you mean?" I asked.

"You heard the kid that just testified," Barbara responded, waving a piece of her sandwich. "He saw him do it!"

"You know," Jonathan said, somewhat sheepishly. "We really aren't supposed to discuss the case."

"The judge did tell us that," Laura said.

"Judge, smudge," Barbara responded. "I'm talking to you guys. It's not like I'm talking to the press. We've got to talk about it eventually."

"The judge said we're all supposed to keep an open mind," Laura said. "We haven't even heard the defense's side."

Eric J. Lee

"There's no side. There's just the truth. He's guilty. I can tell. He's got those beady little eyes. Just like my ex-husband." Everyone looked at each other, too surprised and shocked by Barbara's speech to interrupt. "Don't get me wrong," Barbara said, pausing for a moment to try to finish chewing. "I'm pretty well off now, but I had a tough childhood. I know Paul's kind. He's spoiled rotten. He probably..."

"That's not true," Catherine said, interrupting Barbara's rant. "He grew up in a poorer neighborhood. He has worked hard to get to where he is today." I wondered how Catherine knew this, but I didn't ask her because I wanted the subject to be changed.

Laura seemed rather upset with Barbara's prejudging. I shook my head at Laura as if to say, "Let it go." She obviously wanted to say something, but took my advice to remain silent.

Soon after lunch, we were back in the courtroom and seated in the jury box. The judge welcomed us back before turning his attention to the defense table. "The defense will now cross-examine Alan Clark." Alan took the stand again.

The defense attorney approached Alan who appeared intimidated at the prospect of being cross-examined. "Alan Clark," the defense attorney began. I feared for the teenager. "You said you went to a party the night Gary Bender was robbed and murdered?"

"Yes, I did," Alan responded cautiously, his eyes trained on the defense attorney.

"Alan, you took an oath to tell the truth. But when the prosecuting attorney asked you about the party you went to, you said there was no beer there. Isn't that untrue?"

"No, I didn't say that. I said I didn't drink beer. I don't like beer. But, there was some at the party."

"Some? Wasn't there so much drinking at this party that after only two hours, you and Brad Logan had to leave to make a beer run at Buckley Liquors."

Alan paused. "I wouldn't call it a beer run."

The defense attorney rolled her eyes before turning to look at the judge. She indicated that she wanted to introduce a videotape as Defense Exhibit A. The judge nodded and the defense attorney turned back to Alan. "I will re-ask the question. But, before I do, I want you to know that this videotape is from the hidden camera at Buckley Liquors. You see, the same video camera which showed the robbery caught you and Brad Logan purchasing not one, but two cases of beer."

As the defense attorney put the tape in the VCR, Nancy feverishly wrote in her notepad. David leaned over to me and jokingly asked me if I had any popcorn. The videotape was far from exciting. It showed Alan and another teenage boy, a little bit bigger, buying two cases of beer. I did notice something strange. The kid with Alan paid some money to the cashier, Gary Bender. Gary took the money and then motioned for more.

The tape ended and the defense attorney walked back to Alan. "Was that you and your friend, Brad Logan on that videotape?"

"Yes, but I still wouldn't call it a beer run. We only went once."

"How old are you?"

"Seventeen."

"And your friend Brad?"

"He's seventeen also."

"Do you know how old you have to be to legally buy beer?"

"Yeah," Alan said with a sigh. "Twenty-one."

"So, you illegally purchased..."

"Objection!" the prosecuting attorney exclaimed as he rose from his seat. "This line of questioning is completely irrelevant."

Eric J. Lee

"Your honor," the defense attorney said. "My questions are directed to the state of mind of the witness when he alleges that he saw the defendant commit the crime."

"Overruled!" the judge said. "Answer the question."

Alan looked confused. "Could you repeat the question?"

"So, after you illegally bought the beer, you went outside to make a phone call when you supposedly saw the defendant drive up. What time was that?"

"About 11:30 at night."

"11:30 at night," the defense attorney repeated, turning to the jury. "About how far did you say you were from the car when you think you saw Paul Sutton?"

Alan thought for a few seconds. "About 25 feet, roughly."

"Alan, I propose it is impossible to identify a person twenty-five feet away at 11:30 at night."

"It wasn't completely dark. There are some big overhead lights at Buckley Liquors."

The defense attorney shook her head. "This just doesn't make sense, Alan. Maybe if we recreate it on the diagram, I could understand." She brought back People's Exhibit 3, the diagram of Buckley Liquors. "Now, you said you recognized the car first, then the scratch on it, and then the defendant. Is that correct?"

"Yes, that's right," Alan said, doing his best to follow her questions.

"When did you first notice what you claim is the defendant's car?"

"I first noticed it on Addison Street before he made a right hand turn into Buckley Liquors. I was waiting for Brad to get off the phone. I happened to be looking that way."

"So, you knew it was the defendant's car before it even got to the parking lot?"

"No," Alan said slowly. "I just noticed a car on the street. It wasn't until it was in the lighted parking lot that I could tell it was a Porsche 914 and had a scratch which made me sure it was Mister Sutton's car."

The defense attorney looked at the diagram. "At what point did you notice the scratch? Before or after the car came to a stop?"

Alan paused a moment, looking up at the ceiling as he thought. "Before," Alan said, now looking directly at the defense attorney. "Just as the car was moving into the parking space."

"Okay," she said, taking a step closer to Alan. "I want to talk about the small scratch. How can you make the leap that because you think you see some scratch, it must be the defendant's car. Is it possible that another car could have a similar scratch?"

"Yes, I suppose it's possible."

"And isn't it possible that Mister Sutton had painted over the scratch on his car?"

"Not really. I saw him the morning of the murder. I was walking to school and I saw the car and Mister Sutton at a gas station close to school. I remember seeing the scratch."

"All right," the defense attorney said, with a wave of her hand. "You think you see a scratch which you admit is possible that could appear on another car. And you notice this scratch before the car comes to a stop. When did you think you recognized the defendant?"

"When I saw the mark, I knew it his car. So, I naturally looked at the driver to see if it was him. When the car came to a stop, I was sure. It was Mister Sutton."

"And when you realized it was Mister Sutton, you immediately ducked and told Brad to duck because you didn't want Mister Sutton to see you. Isn't that correct?"

"That's right."

"Okay, Alan, let's think about this for a moment. How many seconds elapsed from the time you realized there was a scratch on the car to the moment you identified the driver as Mister Sutton?"

"Not long at all. I'd guess three, four seconds."

"And then you immediately ducked down, right?"

"That's right."

"Okay. Let's try to get a mental picture of what's going on. You don't want Mister Sutton to see you, because after all you and your friend just broke the law. Right?"

"Yeah," Alan said with a slight shoulder shrug.

"Okay, you don't want him to see you. You identify a car that looks like his. You even see a mark like the one on his car. In your mind, you're sure it's the defendant's car. And three seconds later you duck in fear." The defense attorney paused a moment as she rested her left hand on the railing of the witness box. "Isn't it possible, Alan, since you were so concerned about being seen, you saw what you think is the defendant's car and ducked out of the way before you really got a good look at the driver? Isn't that possible?"

Alan looked a little confused as his forehead wrinkled. "No, I'm sure. I saw him."

"How can you be so sure? It was at night. You just said you only looked at the driver for three or four seconds. Three seconds! It's not possible you ducked thinking it was Mister Sutton because you were convinced it was his car, you didn't want to risk being seen, and thus you never really got a good look at the driver?"

"No, I looked into the car and saw Mister Sutton before I ducked."

"Alan, I don't understand how you can be so sure."

"Objection, your honor," the prosecutor said, rising. "Defense counsel is continuing to ask variations on the same question. The witness has already stated what he saw and the circumstances around what he saw. The defense is badgering the witness."

"Sustained," the judge ruled, with little thought.

"I withdraw the question," the defense attorney said, raising her left hand, but keeping her eyes trained on Alan. "I'm sorry Alan. It's just that it didn't make sense to me that you could be sure unless you have some reason to want Mister Sutton to be guilty."

"Objection! Motion to strike. The defense has no evidence for this accusation."

"Do you have a reason to dislike Mister Sutton?!" the defense attorney asked loudly, only a few feet from the teenager.

"Objection, your honor!"

The judge pounded his gavel. "Order in this court room!" The courtroom quickly became quiet and Alan appeared a little flustered. "The objection is sustained. Ladies and gentlemen of the jury, you will disregard the defense's last question. Now, counsel to the bench." Both attorneys approached the judge. The judge did most of the talking and it was directed at the defense attorney.

Once the conference ended, the defense attorney said, "No further questions."

The prosecutor who did not re-question Buckley or Ms. Andersen felt the need to do so with Alan. "Alan, the defense attorney implied you might lie to the police about seeing Mr. Sutton. Would that be correct?"

"No. I did see Mister Sutton that night."

"Now, Alan. Are you sure you saw Mr. Sutton's car pull up to Buckley Liquors?"

"Positive, it had the exact same model, color and it had been keyed above the right tire." Alan added forcefully, "It was the same car."

"Are you absolutely sure it was Mr. Sutton who was in the car?"

"Yes, I'm absolutely sure." The prosecutor said that he had no further questions. But what was surprising was that the defense attorney did not subject Alan to recall as she did with Buckley and Ms. Anderson. So, Alan would not be back to testify. I guess the defense did not want the jury to be reminded of Alan's testimony.

There was a short pause in the court as the prosecutor looked over his notes for a second. He then stood and announced that the people would like to call Brad Logan to the stand. A six foot, muscular teenager walked into the courtroom as if he had a chip on his shoulder. He had a strange grin, but also a confident, almost arrogant look on his face. He wore brand new blue jeans and a collarless shirt. After he was sworn in, the prosecutor asked him to identify Mr. Paul Sutton. Brad was able to do that. Brad went on to explain that he knew Paul Sutton because Mr. Sutton taught his Geometry class. Brad then recalled the events that took place the night Gary Bender was robbed and murdered.

"So, me and Alan, we went to pick up some beer at Buckley Liquors," Brad said.

"Your friend, Alan Clark," the prosecutor said. "Does he drink?"

"Who? Alan," Brad said with a snicker. "No way. He never touches the stuff."

"And you?"

"Little bit, but I know how to keep it under control."

"And what happened after you arrived at Buckley Liquors?"

"We bought the beer and went outside to make a phone call."

"Who did you call?"

"I wanted to call this girl and find out why she wasn't at the party. We were only a few blocks away from her house. I was thinking we could walk by her house to pick her up."

So, what happened when you called her?" the prosecutor asked.

"Well, I was talking to her when Alan hit me on the shoulder and told me to duck."

"Did you duck?"

"Yeah, I could tell Alan was serious. I hung up the phone and dove to the ground. When I was down on the ground, I asked him what was going on and he told me Mister Sutton had just pulled up."

"What happened next?"

"Well, I heard a car door slam and I peered out and saw Mister Sutton walk into the liquor store."

"Did you get a look at his car?"

"Yeah. While he was in the liquor store, I got a real good look at it. It was definitely Mister Sutton's car. I saw the key mark above the right front tire."

"You saw the key mark on the car that pulled into the parking lot?"

"Yes." Brad explained, as Alan had before him, that he then heard gunshots, ducked back behind the phone booth, and saw the defendant race out of the store and nearly run over a lady walking her dog as he peeled out of the parking lot.

"Brad, you're testifying to seeing a lot of things. So, I have to ask you. How's your vision?"

"20/20. I've always had good vision. I took an eye test three months ago."

"No further questions," the prosecutor said before the judge suggested a five minute break before Brad would be cross examined.

The jurors slowly left the courtroom and the building, needing a breath of fresh air. I was outside talking to David and Catherine when Barbara came over to interrupt. "I told you he was guilty," Barbara whispered to the three of us. "That other kid, uh, Brad saw him do it too."

Eric J. Lee

"Really, we shouldn't be talking about the case, especially this close to the courtroom," I said. Barbara shrugged and walked away.

The jurors again took their seats in the courtroom and the defense attorney approached Brad Logan, who was slouched in the witness chair.

"Brad, do you play any sports at your high school?"

There was a long pause as if Brad was hoping the prosecuting attorney would object. "Yeah, football."

"Would you say you're very good?"

"I've had my moments," Brad said with a smirk.

"Well, according to your yearbook, you were voted MVP in football during your freshman and sophomore years."

"Objection, your honor," the prosecutor said. "Irrelevant."

The defense attorney turned to the judge. "Your honor, I will show relevance. This line of questioning goes toward bias." The judge overruled the objection and the defense attorney continued. "Now being an MVP two years in a row and the leading rusher, you must have serious thoughts about playing college ball."

"Yeah, I hope I can play somewhere."

"Now, after great freshman and sophomore years, how did you do this past season, as a junior?"

"I didn't play," Brad mumbled.

"What was that? I didn't hear you."

"I said I didn't play," Brad said slowly and clearly.

"Why didn't you play?"

"My grades weren't good enough to be on the team," Brad said sighing.

"Were you failing any classes?"

"Yeah, a couple."

"Was one of them the geometry class from Mr. Sutton?"

44

"Yeah," Brad responded, straightening up in his seat.

"You must resent Mr. Sutton for keeping you off the team in your important junior year."

"Objection, your honor!" the prosecutor exclaimed. "The defense is putting words in the witness' mouth."

"I'm sorry, your honor," the defense attorney said. She turned back to Brad. "In your own words, how did it make you feel when Mister Sutton refused to change your grade to allow you to play football?"

Brad paused for a second. I think he was gearing himself up to fight off the defense's accusation. "I was upset, but that has nothing to do with what I saw. I saw the car. It had a key mark above the front right tire."

"Yes, the key mark. How do you remember the location of the key mark so well?"

"Because I've seen it many times."

"How could you see it many times?" she asked. "The teacher's lot is on the other side of the school from the student's parking lot. So, when is it that you always see it?"

Brad paused for a moment as he looked at the defense attorney. "Look, I just know Mr. Sutton's car had a key mark, and I saw the key mark on the car that pulled into the parking lot that night."

"That key mark was made the day after Mr. Sutton refused to change your grade despite your pleas and your coach's pleas." The defense attorney put her hands on the witness stand coming eye to eye with Brad. "Isn't it true you keyed Mr. Sutton's car?" Brad simply stared at her. "Isn't that true?" she repeated.

"All right, so I did it," Brad said. "But that doesn't change the fact that I saw him get out of that car that night." I looked over at the prosecutor who was doing his best to hide his frustration.

"Oh, you saw him," the defense attorney said. "Earlier, you said Alan had to tell you that he had seen Mister Sutton because you were on the phone."

"Yeah," Brad said slowly.

"But, Alan admitted he didn't recognize Mr. Sutton until he supposedly brought the car to a stop and fearful that Mr. Sutton might see you two, Alan yelled for you to duck. Didn't you duck immediately?"

"Yeah," Brad replied slowly.

"So, when did you ever see Paul Sutton? Alan said he never saw the defendant's face after he ducked."

"No, I didn't see his face. He had his mask on, but I know what he looks like. I took his class. After the shots, I saw him run out and get in his car."

"Now, let me get this straight," the defense attorney said, walking away from the witness. "It was 11:30 at night. It was dark. You had been drinking earlier that night. You were over 25 feet away. And you're sure it was the defendant whose face you never saw."

"Yeah, I'd swear to it," Brad said. "'Cuz, I saw the key mark on the car when he was in the store."

"Yes, the key mark that you made," the defense attorney remarked before saying she had no further questions.

Brad seemed agitated. As she walked away, Brad yelled, "You can twist things all you want, but I saw him! I know what I..."

"Silence!" the judge commanded as he pounded on his gavel. "Brad Logan's last comments will be stricken from the record and Brad, you will only respond to the questions asked of you." Instead of arguing with the judge, Brad simply displayed his frustration by shaking his head.

The prosecutor said he had no further questions, but the defense attorney wanted Brad to remain subject to recall.

The prosecutor called Jennifer Wells to the stand. Just walking into the courtroom, she appeared different than other witnesses. She didn't appear frightened as Ms. Anderson did, nor was she arrogant like Brad Logan. She appeared confident and serious about her role in the case. She looked to be in her mid-forties and stood about five foot seven.

"Mrs. Wells. What is your place of residence?"

"Kings City."

"Do you have any nighttime habits in which you customarily engage in?"

"Well, almost every night, I walk my dog. I work a late shift and don't get home until about eleven. The first thing I do is change and go for a walk."

"I'd like to take you back to the night of October 15th. Did anything unusual happen on your walk?"

Mrs. Wells said, "I was walking along Addison Street when this red sports car sped out of the parking lot. It nearly ran me over. I had to grab the leash to yank my dog back."

"You said the car came out of a parking lot. What parking lot?"

"Oh, the parking lot at Buckley Liquors," she answered.

"And what time was that?"

"I'd say about eleven thirty, roughly," Mrs. Wells said. The prosecutor nodded before saying that he had no further questions.

Unlike with all of the other witnesses, the defense attorney remained seated at the defense table to cross-examine the witness. "Mrs. Wells, you only said you saw a red car. What was the make of the car?"

"I don't know. It was dark and it all happened so quickly that I couldn't tell. Like I said, I believe it was some kind of sports car."

"I see. Can you tell me if it was an old car or a new car?"

Mrs. Wells paused. "No, I couldn't."

"Did you see any distinguishable marks on the car? Like scratches?"

"No," Mrs. Wells responded, shaking her head.

"Did you get a look at the driver?"

"No. There wasn't any time."

"How about passengers in the car? Could you tell how many other people were in the car?"

"No."

"How about the license plate number?"

"No," Mrs. Wells responded. "As I said, it was dark and it happened so…"

"Mrs. Wells, is it your testimony that you can not identify the driver, the model of the car, any scratches on the car, and the license plate, partially because it was too dark?"

"That is correct."

"No further questions," the defense attorney said.

I quickly skimmed through my notepad to see how many witnesses we've had. There was Jason Buckley, Sallie Anderson, Alan Clark, Brad Logan, and Jennifer Wells. The next witness was a man named Dr. Francis Baculi. He wore glasses over his skinny face and a blue suit over his short body. His hair was short, but completely black which caused me to wonder whether he had dyed his hair. As he sat down, he seemed relaxed and even paused to smile at the jury. The prosecuting attorney entered Dr. Baculi in as an expert in film and videotape. The defense did not challenge this motion.

In the first series of questions, the prosecution established Dr. Baculi as the head of Kings City forensic division who had testified as an expert in forensic science 62 times. The prosecutor picked up People's Exhibit 2. "Have you viewed this videotape, the tape that shows the murder of Gary Bender?"

"Yes, I have," Dr. Baculi answered, with a cough.

"Based on your expertise, do you have an opinion as to whether the murderer was male or female?"

"In my opinion, the figure on the videotape is male."

"Have you visited Buckley Liquors, the scene of the videotape?"

"Yes, I have."

"Did you issue a report on your findings?"

"Yes."

The prosecutor introduced People's Exhibit 4 and 5. People's Exhibit 4 was Doctor Baculi's report and People's Exhibit 5 was a police report. He directed Dr. Baculi to open one of the reports. "According to your report, what was Gary Bender's murderer's weight?"

Dr. Baculi looked down. "Between 155 and 175 pounds". The prosecuting attorney asked him to open and look at the police report, which disclosed the height and weight of the defendant days after the murder. "It states Paul Sutton's weight is 162 pounds."

"So your analysis says the murderer weighed between 155 and 175 and the police report said Paul Sutton weighs 162 pounds," the prosecutor said reviewing. "How about height?"

Dr. Baculi said, as he peered over the top of his glasses, "My report states the murderer was between 5 foot nine and three quarter inches and five feet ten and one half inch."

"Now, your range only covers three quarters of an inch." The prosecuting attorney held up his thumb and index finger as if to approximate three-quarters of an inch. "How can you be so accurate?"

"By analyzing the height of other objects in the store relative to the murderer on the videotape and then measuring those items on the premises, height can accurately be measured. We have the ability to clearly blow up any portion of the videotape approximately ten times its size."

Eric J. Lee

"So, your report said between 5 feet nine and three quarter inches and five feet ten and one half inch."

"Five feet ten and one quarter inch," Dr. Baculi responded, which caused a few murmurs in the courtroom.

"Now, a moment ago, you said that you could blow up the videotape up to ten times the size. Can you demonstrate for the jury what you found?"

"Sure," Dr. Baculi said, walking over to the VCR. With remote control in hand, he played the videotape until the picture froze on the murderer just as he pulled out his gun. "Now, on this frame, we can blow up this picture." Dr. Baculi pressed a button that caused a portion of the screen to enlarge. He made a circular motion on the screen around the murderer's forearm. "You can clearly see a hanging thread, about a half inch long, coming from the jacket."

Dr. Baculi returned to the witness stand and the prosecutor asked, "Is there any significance to this hanging thread?"

"Yes, it's an unusual flaw in the jacket."

I watched Paul who simply stared at Dr. Baculi showing no emotion. The prosecutor announced that he was introducing People's Exhibit 6. "Do you know what this is?"

"Yes," Dr. Baculi said, taking hold of a jacket. "A few days after the murder, a Kings City policeman found this jacket in the defendant's closet. It also has a hanging thread of about ½ inch." He rested the jacket back on his lap. "In my opinion, it is the same jacket from the videotape." The prosecutor announced he had no further questions.

The defense attorney stood up and walked up to Dr. Baculi. "I'll take the jacket back." Dr. Baculi handed her the jacket, and she gave it to the clerk before slowly returning back to the witness. "Doctor Baculi, I would like to talk to you about your ranges for weight and height in your report. First, weight. Your report gives a range from 155 to 175 pounds. Twenty pounds is a large range. Why couldn't you narrow it down?"

50

"Well, unlike height, we can't rely as heavily on other objects on the videotape. Also the man on the videotape was wearing a baggy jacket."

"I see," the defense attorney. "That baggy jacket you're referring to is covering the robber's forearms, shoulders, chest and stomach. That's what makes it so difficult, right?"

"That's correct."

"Well, we're just going to have to live with the 155 and 175 range then. According to your own report, what percent of men in the U.S. weigh between 155 and 175 pounds?"

"About 45%."

"Hmmm, 45%," the defense attorney said. "So, there are currently about 250 million adults in the United States. Do you think that is a reasonable assumption?"

Dr. Baculi paused a moment before nodding. "Yes, that's about right."

"Now, using an estimate of 48% of those people are men, that would mean there are over 120 million men in the United States. And according to you, 45% of the men are between 155 and 175 pounds, that leaves over 54 million men that fit into your range." She walked back to the defense table to pick up a calculator. "54 million is such a big number it is hard to get a handle on it. A football stadium may seat 60,000 people. To get 54 million people, you would have to fill nine hundred stadiums. Nine hundred! So, there are nine hundred football stadiums full of men who fit in your weight interval."

"You are talking about the entire U.S., but the murder happened in Kings City," Dr. Baculi said.

"Believe it or not, people from all the country come and leave Kings City."

"Objection, your honor," the prosecutor said. "Argumentative."

Eric J. Lee

"Sustained." The judge looked annoyed. "Stick to asking the witness questions, and Doctor Baculi, you will only answer the questions that are asked of you."

Doctor Baculi nodded as the defense attorney turned back to him. "Okay, let's talk about height. About what percent of the men in the U.S. are between the height of five feet nine and three quarter inches and five feet ten and one half inch?"

"Well, that would be about 9%," Dr. Baculi said.

The defense attorney looked at her calculator. "That would mean there are about 20 million men between those heights in the U.S. That's about 333 football stadiums. Correct?"

Dr. Baculi glanced at the judge before finally commenting, "That's correct."

"All right," the defense attorney said, putting down her calculator. "We have established there are literally millions of people who fit in your ranges. Let's talk about the people who don't. Let's say, hypothetically, someone who is shorter, say five foot eight, wears higher heeled shoes. Or maybe someone who is skinny puts something under his baggy jacket to look more like the defendant." As the defense attorney spoke, she slowly approached Dr. Baculi. "Is that possible? Someone who isn't in your intervals, could that person impersonate the defendant and thus fall into your intervals?"

Dr. Baculi dipped his head. "Possible? Yes, I suppose it's possible. But, that would pre-suppose someone would know the defendant's exact measurements."

"But, it is possible. Right?"

"Yes."

Feeling that she had made her point, the defense attorney said she had no further questions.

The prosecuting attorney rose from his chair and asked Dr. Baculi questions from behind his desk. "The defense questioned you about the population of the United States. However, I want to talk to you about simple percentages. That is the basis of your report, right?"

"That's correct," Dr. Baculi responded.

"Okay," the prosecutor said slowly. "Your report concluded three things. One, the murderer is male. Two, the murderer weighed between 155 and 175 pounds. Three, the murderer's height is between five feet nine and three quarter inches and five feet ten and one half inch. And upon subsequent review of the police report, you know the defendant meets all the criteria, right?"

"Yes, that's right."

"What are the chances, according to your report, of a person meeting all three criteria?"

"About five percent."

"Only five percent, one in twenty people. So, to put it another way, if there were someone else who committed this crime, other than the defendant, what are the random chances that person would happen to meet all three of these criteria?"

"Five percent," Dr. Baculi said, adjusting his glasses.

The prosecutor said, "I have no further questions." I was mildly surprised when the defense did not hold Dr. Baculi for recall.

The prosecution's next witness was Sgt. James Griffin. He walked with a slight limp as he approached the witness stand. A short, portly man in his forties, Sgt. Griffin wore a brown uniform and, showing proper respect to the court, held his brown hat in his hand. Without his hat, his receding hairline was plainly visible. The prosecution established that he headed the investigation in this case for the Kings City Police department. The prosecutor then asked, "When did you first suspect Paul Sutton murdered Gary Bender?"

"Mr. Sutton became a suspect on Friday, the night of the murder after questioning Alan Clark and Brad Logan."

"So, did you attempt to question Paul Sutton that night?"

"We tried," Sgt. Griffin said. "But, there was no answer at his house."

"So, what did you do?"

"We tried again on Saturday morning, but he wasn't there. So, we reached his family to see if they knew his whereabouts. His brother, a Mr. Shawn Sutton, told us he was on vacation with his wife for their wedding anniversary. Shawn expected him back sometime Sunday evening."

"Did Paul come back Sunday evening?"

"Yes, he did. We questioned him Sunday night. We got a search warrant to search his home and we searched it on Monday morning."

"What did you find during your search of the defendant's home?"

"In the defendant's closet, we found a Chicago Bulls jacket."

The prosecutor picked up the Chicago Bulls jacket from the clerk's desk. He walked back over to the witness stand. "Is this the jacket that you confiscated during your search of the defendant's house?"

"Yes, it is," Sgt. Griffin responded.

"Is there anything that distinguishes this jacket from other Chicago Bulls jackets?"

"Yes. There's a hanging thread, which matched the jacket on the videotape." The prosecutor turned toward the jury before stating that he had no further questions.

The defense attorney approached Sgt. Griffin. "During your extensive search of Paul Sutton's house, did you find the murder weapon?"

"No," Sgt. Griffin responded.

"Did you find any guns at all?"

"No."

"On the videotape, we can see that the murderer is wearing a mask. Did you find a mask at the defendant's house during your search?"

"No."

"In the video, the murderer shot Gary Bender and then inspected the body. Did you find the victim's blood on the jacket or on any of the defendant's clothes?"

"No," Sgt. Griffin said, slightly shifting in his seat.

"How about the defendant's hair fibers? Did you find any on the victim?"

"No."

"So, during your extensive search, you didn't find the murder weapon. You didn't find a mask. You didn't find any guns. You didn't find any blood evidence or hair fibers. All you found was a Chicago Bulls jacket?"

"Yes, that's correct." Sgt. Griffin swiveled in his chair a bit. A trace of discomfort appeared in his otherwise composed demeanor.

"All that you found was a jacket from the Chicago Bulls," the defense attorney repeated, shaking her head. "The Bulls are a very popular team. A team that plays in a city not more than five hundred miles from Kings City. Isn't that correct?"

"That's right."

"No further questions," the defense attorney said before taking a seat. The prosecution decided not to question Sgt. Griffin further and the defense attorney did not elect to hold him subject to recall.

The prosecution called another policeman, Officer Brian Cummings to the stand. Dressed in full uniform, he looked to be in his late thirties. He was a tall and muscular man. As he approached the stand, he appeared to be all business.

"Officer Cummings. Who do you work for?"

"Stanislaus Police Force."

"What were you doing late on the night of October 15th?"

"I was working the late shift, patrol car."

The prosecutor introduced People's Exhibit 7. It was a small sheet of paper. He handed it to the witness and asked him what it was.

"It's a traffic ticket," Officer Cummings responded.

"Who wrote the ticket and who got the ticket?"

"I wrote it up, and a Mister Paul Sutton got the ticket," Officer Cummings said, reading the ticket.

"This is important. Are you sure it was Mister Sutton who was driving?"

"Positive. With every traffic stop, I observe the picture ID of the driver on his driver's license. See, near the top left of the ticket, I wrote the driver's license number," Officer Cummings said, pointing to the traffic ticket. "That's Paul Sutton's driver's license number."

"Does the ticket indicate the date and time of the violation?"

He looked at the ticket. "It was 1:55 AM on October 16th."

"I see. Does the ticket also have the license plate number of the vehicle that Mister Sutton was driving?"

"Yes," the officer responded, looking down at the ticket. He read off the license number.

"And does that license number match any car that Paul Sutton owns?"

"Yes, his Porsche 914."

"Exactly where did the violation take place?"

"On Main Street, near the Exxon gas station in South Stanislaus, just off Highway 5," Officer Cummings replied.

"Let me make sure I understand this," the prosecutor said. "If someone were to drive from Kings City to Stanislaus on Highway 5, they would drive right past this particular gas station?"

"Basically. It is less than a quarter mile off Highway 5. You can see the sign from the highway."

"Do you know how long, driving the speed limit, it would take to drive from Stanislaus to Kings City using the highway?"

Officer Cummings twisted in his chair slightly. "About an hour and a half. Maybe a little less."

"Do you remember the violation? And, if so, can you tell the court what happened?"

"Well, I was parked at the corner of Main and Liberty. I saw Mister Sutton getting gas at the gas station. Then, I observed him pull out and run straight through a red light."

"Did Mister Sutton appear to be in a hurry?"

"Yes," Officer Cummings replied.

The prosecutor said that he had no further questions.

The defense attorney slowly stood up and from behind her desk, said, "I only have a couple of questions for you at this time. In what city did this violation take place?"

"Stanislaus," Officer Cummings replied.

"Stanislaus. Not Kings City. How far is Kings City from the place that you issued the violation?"

Officer Cummings paused a moment, looking up at the ceiling. "About 90 miles, roughly."

"90 miles," the defense attorney repeated. "No further questions." She decided to hold Officer Cummings subject to recall.

The prosecuting attorney announced that he had no further questions and surprisingly, had no more witnesses to call. The prosecution had rested. The judge decided to delay the start of the defense's case until tomorrow. He gave us our usual instructions to avoid discussing the case, keep an open mind, and refrain from conducting any of our own investigations.

I said a quick good-bye to David and Laura and walked to my car. As I drove home, I thought about the prosecution's duty-- to prove that the defendant is guilty beyond a reasonable doubt. Was I convinced before hearing the other side? Two eyewitnesses swore they saw him. An expert linked the physical characteristics of the defendant to the guilty party on videotape. A jacket was found at his home with the same hanging thread as the one on the videotape. Testimony about a key mark indicated the defendant's car was at the crime scene. That was a lot, but somehow I didn't feel I was seeing the whole picture.

The next morning, I was back in my car, headed to the courthouse. The sun barely shone in the cloudy sky on this Wednesday, January 20th. Although the air was cool and crisp, it was a far cry from the frigid temperatures that Kings City had endured in the previous winters.

The bailiff called us into the courtroom and we all took our seats. To my right, Nancy, completely focused and serious, was ready to go with her notepad. To my left, David looked a little groggy, perhaps not getting enough sleep last night. The judge turned to the defense attorney and reminded her that she had deferred her opening statement at the beginning of the case.

The defense attorney stood up and slowly walked over to the jury. "Ladies and gentlemen of the jury, you have a very important duty-- to decide a man's fate. A man who has never committed a crime in his life. A man who has been hailed by his peers as the best teacher at his high school. A man who had absolutely no motive for the murder the prosecution would like you to believe that he committed. A man who in fact has an alibi at the time of the shooting."

"As a spouse of a senator, Paul Sutton has been thrust in the public eye. And with his wife's re-election bid this November, her political rivals have engaged in a desperate, smear campaign. There is no other decision but "not guilty" to arrive at because there is not enough evidence to prove him guilty beyond a reasonable doubt. I repeat, beyond a reasonable doubt. That's the law and that's the standard, ladies and gentlemen."

"The defense would like to call Mr. Perry King to the stand," the defense attorney announced. A man in his early fifties with black, wavy hair walked up to the witness stand. He wore a gray suit with matching gray and white tie. Fit and healthy for a man of his age, he seemed relaxed and comfortable as he crossed his legs in the witness chair.

"What do you do for a living?" the defense attorney asked.

"I'm principal of Kings City High School," Mr. King said.

"How long have you known the defendant, Paul Sutton?"

"He was teaching here when I became principal five years ago."

"What are your impressions of him as a teacher?"

"He's fabulous," Mr. King said, smiling. "You know, he won teacher of the year two years ago. He's great with the kids, stays late after school and helps some of the kids who are having problems."

"How about as a person?"

"He's a great guy."

"Do you think Paul Sutton would be capable of a violent murder?"

"No way. He is about the nicest, most gentle person I have ever met."

"Well, do you know who Brad Logan is?"

"Yeah, he's a student at our school."

"Do you know all of the students at your school?"

"No. It's a big school. I only know students who are high profile or have disciplinary problems."

"And which is Brad?"

"Both, actually," Mr. King said. "He's a great football player. Everyone in school knows him for that. But, he's definitely got a discipline problem and a horrible temper. He blew his top when he was dropped from the football team because of his grades. He and his coach came into my office mad as heck. They wanted me to put pressure on Paul Sutton to change Brad's grade."

"And did you?"

"No. That's not the way I operate."

"Brad says that he saw Mr. Sutton enter the liquor store and kill the cashier. Do you think Brad was so mad at Mr. Sutton for not letting him on the team that he would fabricate..."

"Objection, your honor," the prosecutor said, rising. "Lack of foundation. Calls for speculation."

"Sustained," the judge said immediately as he apparently jotted down a note. The judge glared authoritatively at the defense attorney. As if she had sensed the judge's disposition, the defense attorney said that she had no further questions, and returned to her seat.

The prosecutor approached the witness. "Do you know Alan Clark?"

"Yes, I do. He's a junior at the high school."

"Do you know him because he has a disciplinary problem?"

"Oh no," Mr. King said. "Alan is high profile because he participates in student government."

"So, in your experience, Alan Clark has been a good, honest student."

"I guess so," Mr. King said, shrugging his shoulders. With that, the prosecutor announced that he had no further questions and opted not to hold Mr. King subject to recall.

"At this time, the defense would like to re-call Brad Logan." Brad entered the courtroom escorted by the bailiff. When Brad stood up to be sworn in, he didn't appear eager to return. As he took his seat, he appeared to have a chip on his shoulder.

"Brad, your principal, Perry King, just testified that after the defendant refused to raise your math grade, you and your coach went to his office and demanded your grade be changed."

"We discussed, not demanded."

"Yesterday, you said you were so mad that your discussions were unsuccessful, you took a key and scraped Mr. Sutton's new car. Isn't that correct?"

"Objection, your honor," the prosecuting attorney said, rising. "The witness already admitted to keying the defendant's car. This line of questioning is irrelevant and redundant."

"Sustained," the judge said.

"Brad, would it be fair to say that you were so mad at Mister Sutton for losing your important junior year of football that you're trying to frame him for a crime that you know..."

"Objection! Motion to strike!" the prosecutor exclaimed. "She's badgering the witness. It is Paul Sutton, not Brad Logan who is on trial here."

"Sustained," the judge said. He turned to the court reporter and instructed her to strike the defense's last question from the record. He warned the defense attorney that the court would not tolerate such questions.

"I'm sorry, your honor," the defense attorney said before returning her attention to Brad. "About five minutes before Gary Bender was murdered, you bought two cases of beer."

"Yeah," Brad said.

The defense attorney nodded. "Yes, we all know that because we saw it on Defense Exhibit A." The defense attorney picked up a videotape and put it in the VCR, which was pointed toward the jury. It was the same evidence that we saw before. Brad and Alan were buying the beer from Gary on video with no soundtrack. The whole clip ran about thirty-five seconds. Again, the only strange thing was that Gary had to motion for more money after Brad had handed him the original sum.

The defense attorney stopped the tape and asked Brad, "How much do two cases of beer usually cost?"

"About twenty-five bucks."

"On the videotape, we can see you paying a certain amount. Then, Gary seemed to insist for more. And you gave him another bill. Why? Didn't you know how much the beer cost?"

Brad shifted in his seat and glanced at the prosecutor for help, which he got. "Objection, your honor. This line of questioning is completely irrelevant to the case at hand."

The judge looked up at the ceiling, perhaps to contemplate the disagreement between the two attorneys. Before he made a ruling, the defense attorney added, "I believe the events that happened five minutes before the crime between the victim and a key prosecution witness are very relevant."

"Overruled," the judge said. He turned to Brad. "You will answer the question."

"The extra money was a bribe. We were underage and Gary knew it. So, we had to pay a little extra."

The defense attorney shook her head. "Just one more question. Do you think bribing someone so you can illegally buy alcohol makes you an honest and trustworthy person?"

Brad looked at the defense attorney, gritting his teeth as he pondered his response. "I'm telling the truth."

"You didn't answer the question, but that's okay. We'll let the jury decide."

A clearly agitated Brad seemed to bite his lower lip, but somehow remained silent. The defense attorney paused, apparently hoping Brad would react. When he didn't, she announced that she had no further questions. The prosecuting attorney didn't want to re-question Brad, perhaps feeling it best to get him off the stand.

The defense attorney called a man named Shawn Sutton. He looked remarkably similar to the defendant. He was of average height; I'd say about five foot ten and average weight for that height. I'd guess that he was in his late thirties. He was clean-shaven just like the defendant, but his hair was slightly longer than Paul's. As he walked to the witness stand, he appeared calm and serious. He was sworn in and the defense attorney asked him if he knew the defendant.

"Yes, he's my brother," Shawn responded calmly.

"Is he older than you?"

"Yes, he's older, by about a year and a half."

"How close are you and your brother?"

"We're very close," Shawn replied immediately. "We've been close my entire life."

"What kind of person is Paul Sutton?"

"He is the nicest, most caring person I know."

"You mean he cares about his friends and family?"

"Well, yes he does," Shawn said. "His close friends and family are very important to him. But when I said that he cares about people, I meant he cares about everyone he meets, whether they're strangers on the street or the many students in his classes."

"Does he care about money?"

"No, not really," Shawn said, scratching behind his ear. "I mean, if he did, he never would have become a high school teacher. I mean, he has a Ph.D. He could have gotten a much higher paying job if money were so important."

"Where did you two grow up?"

"In a city called Pinewoods. We lived in the same house for over thirteen years. It wasn't the best of neighborhoods. But, we had a home."

"How big was the house?"

Eric J. Lee

"Pretty small. It was a one-bedroom home. Dad slept in the bedroom and Paul and I shared the living room as our bedroom."

"Was your family in need of money?"

"Yes," Shawn said, nodding. "I mean, our mom died when I was six and our dad worked at the post office. He didn't make that much money."

"So, Paul was certainly in need of money back then," the defense attorney surmised. "To your knowledge, in the thirteen years that you lived in this small house in a bad neighborhood, did Paul ever try to rob or steal anything from anyone?"

"Never. We were taught from the very beginning that was wrong."

"Let me talk to you a little about guns. Does Paul like guns?"

"No, he hates them. Always has."

"So, to your knowledge he doesn't own a gun?"

"No. I've never even seen him hold a gun."

"Shawn. Does anyone know Paul better than you?"

"I don't think so. I've known him for thirty-seven years."

"I have a very important question for you since you know Paul so well and for so long. Do you think Paul Sutton is capable of committing this crime?"

"Absolutely not," Shawn sternly replied before the defense attorney said she had no further questions.

The prosecutor slowly approached the stand. "Moments ago, you said that Paul Sutton was not capable of committing this murder. Were you with him on the night of October fifteenth?"

"No," Shawn said, shifting in his seat. "I wasn't."

"So, when you say he's not capable of this crime, it's not based on any facts that would make it impossible?"

"It's based on the fact that I've known him very personally over the past thirty-seven years." Shawn tapped his index finger

64

on the armrest as he talked. "I know my brother's morals. I know the way my brother thinks. And I know the way my brother acts. He didn't do this."

The prosecuting attorney walked closer to the witness stand. "But since you weren't with him the night of the 15th, you can't say for sure that he didn't commit this crime." Shawn glared at him as he shifted in his seat again. "Can you?"

"No."

The prosecutor decided to end with that, stating that he had no further questions. He did not hold Shawn subject to recall.

It was 10:20 a.m. and the judge called for a short break, which I used to mail a few bills at the post office. We reconvened back in the courtroom at 10:40 a.m. David asked if I had plans for lunch. I shook my head as the judge called the court to order. The defense attorney stood up and announced that she was calling Paul Sutton, the defendant, to the stand. There was a chilling silence as Paul slowly walked to the stand. All eyes and cameras in the courtroom were focused on Paul. I had wondered if he would testify at all. So, it was a surprise to see him called as the fourth witness. I wondered whether this was the last witness the defense would call. "Here we go," I thought, turning to a new page in my notebook.

In his late thirties, Paul was at least seven years younger than his politically-minded wife. He seemed a little overwhelmed and befuddled with the entire situation. He was about five-ten, average build and weight. He looked like the type of teacher you'd want for your child, clean-shaven and well-dressed in a blue sport jacket. He wiped off a little sweat from his brow. I'm sure that he realized his testimony could very well have life or death consequences.

The defense attorney asked, "Paul, have you ever been suspected of murder before this case?"

"No," Paul said while shaking his head.

"How about robbery?"

"No."

"Do you own a gun?"

"No."

"Have you ever even shot a gun?"

"No."

"Paul, you took a solemn oath to tell the truth. Did you on the night of October 15th shoot and kill Gary Bender, the cashier at Buckley Liquors?"

"No," Paul answered emphatically.

"Did you try to rob Buckley Liquors that night?"

"No."

"At any time on October 15th, did you even enter the premises of Buckley Liquors?"

"No."

"Where were you then on the night of Friday, October 15th, the night the prosecution alleges you shot and robbed Gary Bender?"

"That night, I was in Stanislaus."

"How long did you plan to stay in Stanislaus?"

"The whole weekend. It was our wedding anniversary. A friend of mine, Pete Kelly, manages a small resort in Stanislaus. We stayed there."

When the defense attorney asked Paul what he and his wife did when they arrived, he said they met his friend Pete Kelly, got settled in their room, had dinner at a restaurant across the street from the hotel, went for a walk, and then a romantic night in their suite. Paul said that he only left the hotel room once that night, about 1:30 in the morning to get a bottle of wine.

"Where were you around 11:30 that night?"

"I was in bed with my wife," Paul said firmly.

"What car did you take up to Stanislaus?"

"My car, the Porsche 914," Paul responded as I listened with great interest.

"So there's no way your Porsche 914 ever was at Buckley liquors that night?"

"There's no way. I drove my Porsche to school that day in King's City. But, after school I drove the car home, picked up my wife and drove the car directly to Stanislaus." Paul paused for a moment. "At 11:30 at night, my Porsche 914 was parked outside Pete Kelly's resort in Stanislaus."

At that point, the defense attorney appeared to switch gears. "Paul, are you in dire need of money?"

"Of course not. My wife is a senator."

"Did you know Gary Bender?"

"No, not really. I mean, I've been in Buckley Liquors before and seen him, but I didn't know him by name."

"Did he know you?"

"I don't think so."

"One more question," the defense attorney said slowly. "Do you find it incomprehensible that you are being charged for robbery, when you're obviously in no need of money, and for the murder of someone you didn't even know?"

"Definitely," Paul said before the defense attorney said that she had no further questions.

The prosecutor stood up and said that he was introducing People's Exhibit 8. He showed it to the defense attorney and the clerk marked it as evidence. "Mister Sutton, this is Gary Bender's phone bill over the last three years. Highlighted are over fourteen phone calls to your home over the last three years, including one call made October 8th, one week before he was murdered." He handed Paul the exhibit and Paul looked through the piles of pages. "How do you explain fourteen phone calls from a person you didn't know?"

"I don't know," Paul responded, shrugging his shoulders. "He never called me." Paul paused as he searched for an answer. "Maybe he liked to prank call, or maybe he just conducted phone surveys."

The prosecutor shook his head. "One phone call was thirty six minutes. The one on October 8th, that was fifteen minutes. Do you usually stay on the phone that long with prank callers?"

Paul looked back down at the phone bills and shook his head. "I can't explain this. All I can tell you is I did not know Gary Bender." Paul handed the phone bills back to the prosecutor.

"Mister Sutton, being a rather famous household, do you and your wife have your phone number listed?"

"Um, no, we don't."

"So, anyone calling your number couldn't just get it out of the phone book or call information. Isn't that correct?"

"Yeah, that's correct."

"So, someone must have given it to him. Right?"

Paul looked a little bothered as the defense attorney shouted an objection due to lack of foundation.

"Sustained," the judge said.

The prosecutor kept his attention focused on the witness, never looking at the judge. "Mister Sutton, these fourteen phone calls from Gary Bender. Could they be to your wife?"

"No, they couldn't be."

"How do you know that?" the prosecutor quickly asked.

"Because I asked her that exact question," Paul said calmly, proving that he can control his emotions better than his brother on the witness stand.

"And your wife wouldn't lie?"

"No, she wouldn't."

"All right, we've established the phone calls weren't to your wife. And she's the only other person who lives with you. Right?"

"Yes."

"So the calls weren't to your wife and you're the only other person who lives there. Someone was talking to Gary Bender on fourteen different occasions with one call lasting thirty-six minutes. How can you possibly say that you don't know him?"

"Objection!" the defense attorney asserted. "He has already answered that question to the best of his ability." The judge agreed, sustaining the objection.

However, the prosecuting attorney continued, exclaiming, "It was an unlisted number! How can you expect this jury to believe that you don't know him?"

"Objection, your honor," the defense attorney said rising. "He's badgering the witness. The witness has repeatedly answered this question."

The prosecutor said, "Your honor, I'm only trying to..."

The judge pounded his gavel. "Silence! Counsel to the bench. Now!" The attorneys approached the judge and they began to whisper. After about forty seconds, the prosecutor walked back over to Paul Sutton and the defense attorney returned to her seat.

"Okay. Let's talk about your second assertion: that you are not in need of any money." He picked up a small stack of papers and said to the judge, "Introducing into evidence Paul Sutton's financial records, as People's Exhibit 9. This exhibit includes his checking and savings account, as well as home and auto loans."

The judge nodded and the prosecutor turned his attention back to Paul, handing him the stack of papers. He paused a moment to allow Paul to look them over. "According to these records, you have a total savings of less than $8,000 and your house and two cars are over 95% mortgaged. Your wife has been a successful politician for years. You have no kids. And you work as a teacher. Where does all your money go?"

"I don't know. I guess we don't save our money very well."

"Apparently not. You and your wife squandered a substantial amount of money. Didn't that make you desperate on the night of the 15th?"

"No. I've been a lot poorer than I am now and I have never committed a crime."

The prosecutor slowly walked behind his desk. "Do you know Alan Clark?"

"Yes, I do. He was a student in my class."

"Just yesterday, you saw him testify that he saw your car pull up to Buckley Liquors and you got out. How do you reconcile this when you claim you and your car were 100 miles away?"

"I don't know. All I can tell you is that I was in Stanislaus at 11:30 p.m. on October 15th. You know, kids today have some imagination."

"Well, Alan did imagine he would buy a Porsche 914. Did you know he admired that car?"

"Yeah, I did," Paul responded. "I saw him the morning of the 15th at a gas station right by the high school. While I was filling up the car with gas, Alan comes by and tells me about how he was going to get a car like that one day. He was fantasizing, which he did a lot."

"Fantasizing aside, you knew he had an interest in Porsche 914s?"

"Interest?" Paul said before shaking his head. "More like an obsession. He thinks he knows everything about that car."

"How do you mean?"

"Oh," Paul said, thinking for a bit. "Like when I was gassing up that morning, he was telling me that Porsche 914s have an airtight gas tank so I shouldn't be topping off my car. Imagine that. A teenager thinks he knows more about a car than its owner. Alan sometimes loses sight of reality."

The prosecutor paused a moment before saying, "But, Mister Sutton, since Alan seems to know some things about your car, it shouldn't surprise you that he knew about the distinguishable key mark above your front left tire?"

"Nothing Alan knows or thinks that he knows about my car would surprise me."

"Okay, I'd like to talk to you about your supposed alibi. You would like this court to believe you were in Stanislaus the entire night of October 15th."

"I was."

"But, you said you left around 1:30 that night to get some wine."

"I did."

The prosecutor walked back to his table and turned toward the judge. "Request to introduce People's Exhibit 10." The judge nodded and the prosecuting attorney dropped off a copy at the defense table before approaching Paul on the stand. "This is a weather service report on October 15th at midnight in Stanislaus. The temperature outside was 30 degrees, two degrees below freezing." The prosecutor handed it to Paul and paused to let him read the document before saying, "You were in a warm hotel room. Why did you go out in the freezing cold for wine when you could have had some delivered to your room?"

"The hotel didn't have the brand of wine my wife and I had on our wedding night. We both wanted that exact wine. It was supposed to be a special night. I didn't care about the weather," Paul said, handing back the document.

"What brand of wine was it, Mister Sutton?"

"Fetzer Merlot."

"Oh come on, Mister Sutton, that doesn't make any sense. Fetzer Merlot, what's so special about that?"

"It was special to us!" Paul exclaimed, pressing his index finger down on the railing in front of him. Paul paused a moment, as I think he realized that he had inadvertently raised his voice. "When I proposed on the beach, we had Fetzer

Merlot. On our wedding night, we had Fetzer Merlot. We also
had it on our first wedding anniversary. You have to
understand, on really special occasions, enjoying Fetzer Merlot
together is a tradition."

"If it was so important Mister Sutton and so special as you
say, why didn't you get the wine in advance?

"I don't know. I guess I didn't think about it ahead of time."

"Oh come on. You can't have it both ways. You planned
this trip ahead of time. You made the reservation. You were
celebrating your wedding anniversary. Now, how can you tell
this court that it was an important tradition and then completely
forget about it?"

"Objection!" the defense attorney exclaimed. "The witness
has answered the question already. He's badgering the witness."

"Sustained," the judge said.

"Mister Sutton, it was 1:30 in this very cold morning. Was
that honestly the first time you even thought about the wine?
The wine that was so important."

"Yes, it was. We had other things on our minds earlier, if
you know what I mean."

The prosecutor paused a moment. "All right, where did you
go at 1:30 on this very cold morning to get wine?"

"Bill's Liquors," Paul answered.

"Did you call them before you went all the way over there?"

"No, I have..."

"Wait a minute. You didn't call to see if they had Fetzer
Merlot or if they were even open."

"No, I didn't because I had been there three or four times
before. I knew they were open 24 hours and I knew they carried
Fetzer Merlot."

The prosecutor introduced People's Exhibit #11, a detailed
map of Stanislaus, and People's Exhibit #12, a page out of the
Yellow Pages covering the City of Stanislaus. "Okay, Mister
Sutton, you can see Bill's Liquor Store marked and the resort

where you were staying. Also, marked are two other liquor stores: Western Liquors and Big T Liquors. One is west of the resort, the other is a little north." The prosecutor pointed on the map. "But both of the liquor stores were closer than Bill's Liquor Store. Why didn't you go to either of the closer locations?"

"I wasn't aware of them. I live in Kings City, not Stanislaus. I don't know where all the liquor stores are located in Stanislaus."

"Of course, you don't," the prosecutor said, emphasizing the word 'you'. "You don't live in Stanislaus. Which is why you would have looked at this page of the phone book, which was in your room, and found out where the nearest liquor store was. Now, why didn't you do that?"

"Look!" Paul said as he leaned forward in his chair. "I knew where Bill's Liquors was. It was only ten minutes away. I knew how to get there. I knew they were open. And I knew they had Fetzer Merlot. I never even thought of going anywhere else."

The prosecutor seemed to freeze for a moment, apparently stunned by the defendant's answer. He quickly gathered himself. "Come on, isn't the only reason you are saying you went to Bill's Liquors is because that was the liquor store that happened to be close to the spot where you got the ticket. And the fact is that you never went to Bill's Liquor that night. And you actually got that ticket while you were driving back from Kings City, not from Bill's Liquors. And this whole..."

"Objection, your honor," the defense attorney said. "Counsel is not asking a question. He's making a speech!"

"I'll withdraw the question," the prosecutor said with a smirk, before taking a seat.

The defense attorney looked at the prosecuting attorney and shook her head before approaching Paul. She questioned Paul, centering on the fact that he was a respected teacher and law-abiding citizen who wanted to share a rare intimate evening with his well-known wife. It got interesting when the defense attorney introduced a stack of papers into evidence as Defense Exhibit B. "This is a copy of your phone bill for the last three years. Before I ask you a question about these, let me ask you this. Do you know everyone that calls you?"

"Well most," Paul responded, slightly nodding his head. "But, I guess I get my share of wrong numbers, people taking surveys, and people trying to sell something to me. Things like that. So, those people, I obviously wouldn't know."

"How about people you call? Do you know the people you call?"

"Well, yeah," Paul said. "I'm the one making the call."

The defense attorney then explained that Defense Exhibit B's stack of phone bills is from Paul and Gloria Sutton's phone line over the last five years. "Have you reviewed these phone bills?"

"Yes."

"Is there even one phone call to Gary Bender's line?"

"No."

After the defense attorney said that she had no further questions, the prosecution requested that the defendant remain subject to recall. The defendant stepped down from the stand and slowly walked back to his seat next to his attorney. He lovingly touched his wife's hand in the front row behind him before sitting down. The judge looked at his watch. It was 12:10 so he dismissed us for an hour lunch.

As we did yesterday, the jurors assembled outside of the courthouse. Laura suggested that we all try a local Chinese restaurant. Catherine, Barbara, David and I thought it was a good idea. Another juror named Richard Packard joined us as well.

As we walked to the restaurant, I learned Richard was a professor of social science at a local university. He was dressed formally for a juror. He wore slacks and a vest. He was slightly overweight and wore a thinly-trimmed beard.

The seven of us sat down at the table as we all looked at the menu. Like yesterday, Barbara dominated the conversation. She blabbed about her job, the unbelievable cost of buying her new car, and, of course, the case. "Far be it from me to pass judgment, you know, but I don't trust the defendant at all. He says that he was in Stanislaus, yeah, right!"

Of the five of us, only Richard was unaccustomed to Barbara's outspoken comments. Stunned, Richard said, "It sounds like you have already made up your mind. You're supposed to keep an open mind until all of the evidence is in."

"Open mind, my eye!" Barbara exclaimed. "Who goes out for wine at 1:30 in the freaking morning?"

"Excuse me," Laura said. "We really shouldn't be discussing the case." Catherine, David and I shared our agreement, but Barbara just rolled her eyes.

We finished lunch and made our way back to the courtroom. We were let in and the judge called the court to order. "The defense would like to call Gloria Sutton to the stand."

The senator walked to the stand. I believe she was in her mid-forties. An attractive, average height woman, she seemed a little pompous, but keenly aware of what was going on around her. She seemed to command respect and appeared to be a woman who was accustomed to getting what she wanted.

"Gloria," the defense attorney said, addressing the senator by her first name. "Do you know the defendant Paul Sutton?"

"Yes, I do. He's my husband."

"Do you remember the night of October 15th?"

"Yes, I do. Very clearly."

"What did you do that night?"

Gloria told the exact same scenario that Paul had previously told. They left Kings City about 4:30 to celebrate their anniversary at a resort in Stanislaus. They met the hotel manager Pete Kelly, who showed them to their suite. They stayed together in Stanislaus the entire night except when Paul left at 1:30 to pick up Fetzer Merlot.

"Why Fetzer Merlot?" the defense attorney asked. "Couldn't you two have gotten any kind of wine?"

"You have to understand that drinking Fetzer Merlot together has been a tradition. It has come to symbolize something that is very special to us. I was the one who prodded Paul to go out and get some."

"Okay, but why didn't you two look in the phone book to see which store was closest?"

"When Paul agreed to go, he said he knew exactly where to get it. I didn't question him. And I didn't even think about the phone book. Before I knew it, he was out the door."

"You said he left at about 1:30. Could it have been earlier?"

"No, it could not," Gloria said. "I remember mentioning the fact that it was so late."

"How long was he gone?"

"Twenty, thirty minutes at most."

"Now, is it possible to drive from Stanislaus to Kings City and back in thirty minutes?"

"Absolutely not. The two cities are about one hundred miles apart. There's no way he could make that trip in 30 minutes one way, let alone roundtrip."

"Now, the prosecution has stated that Paul is lying because no one would ever leave at 1:30 in the morning to get wine. How do you respond to that?"

"Well, he's not lying because I saw him leave at that time," Gloria said. "I guess what you have to remember is that, for us, 1:30 was not very late. We knew we could stay in bed at the resort all day Saturday if we wanted. Believe me, neither of us were in a hurry to go to sleep."

"So you're absolutely sure your husband was with you, in Stanislaus, at about 11:30 P.M. on the night of October 15th?"

"Yes, I'm one hundred percent sure," Gloria replied. The defense attorney said that she had no further questions.

The prosecutor approached the stand. "Do you love your husband?"

"Of course."

"So, you certainly don't want to see him go to jail?"

"Of course not, but if you're insinuating that I would come to court and lie, you're wrong. I'm only telling the truth."

"Let's talk about your political career. You worked hard to get to where you are today- a United States senator. You've been in politics for over twenty years. Wouldn't your political career be greatly damaged if your husband were convicted of murder?"

"Yes, it would, but so would lying under oath. Everything that I'm testifying to is the truth."

"The truth? Okay. Did you know Gary Bender?"

"No, not really. I've been in that store a couple of times, but I didn't know him."

"Hmm…" the prosecutor said. "I'm confused. Sallie Anderson, Gary's fiancée, said that Gary told her that he knew you."

Gloria flashed a stern look. "All I can tell you is that I did not know him. Many people claim to know someone famous."

"You and Paul live alone, correct?"

"Yes."

"And you have an unlisted number, right?"

"Yes."

The prosecutor brought out People's Exhibit 8, the stack of Gary Bender's bills, and showed Gloria. "So, these fourteen calls by Gary Bender to your household's unlisted number had to be to one of you two." The prosecutor raised his eyebrows and asked, "Were they to you?"

Gloria paused for a second. "No, I told you that I did not know the man."

Feeling that he had made his point, the prosecutor went back to questions implying that the only reason Gloria was testifying was to save her husband and her own political career. The defense objected repeatedly and the prosecutor finally decided to call it quits.

Next to me, David yawned as the defense called a Mr. Pete Kelly to the stand. A slender man in his late fifties raised his right hand to be sworn in. His wavy, brown hair was beginning to turn gray. He wore a collared dress shirt with a red sweater. Just from his expression as he walked to the stand seemed to illustrate a man with a lot of spunk. He didn't appear to be at all frightened with the situation.

"Mister Kelly, how do you know Paul Sutton?"

"Oh, I've been a friend of da family for years," Pete said with an Irish accent. "Known him ever since he was a teenager. I was happy to have Paul and his wife stay at my resort for their anniversary."

"Your resort? Do you own it?"

"Yes, ma'am, I do," Pete responded with a smile. "I also run da front desk."

"What do you do at the front desk?"

"Well, I check folks in and out. Take calls for room service. Take complaint calls. Reservation calls. I might be looking at da books. Not a lot, I suppose."

"On October 15th, did you see Paul Sutton?"

"Yes, I did. He came up about six o'clock to check in. I remember cuz I had just started working da front desk."

"So, you started your shift around six. How long did you stay at the front desk?"

"Until two a.m.," Pete responded. "And it was continuous."

"Now, Mister Kelly. You were at the front desk until 2 AM. Did you see Paul leave his room that night? Say about ten o'clock, the time he would have to leave to get to Kings City by 11:30 PM."

"No," Pete said firmly. "I never saw Paul leave and I never left my post that night." The defense attorney announced that she had no further questions.

"Mister Kelly," the prosecutor said, approaching the stand. "You said you never left the front desk and you worked continuously from six p.m. to two a.m. You are telling this court that you never took a break. Not for dinner or even to go to the restroom?"

Pete smiled, "That's correct. I don't take breaks at the front desk. As far as food goes, if I want something I'll order it and they bring it to the front desk. And there's a restroom right behind da front desk."

"So you could miss someone come or leave while you are in the restroom?"

"Not very likely," Pete said, shaking his head with a smile. "There are bells hooked up to da front door. When the doors are opened, da bells go off. I can hear da bells in the bathroom."

"All right then, did you see Paul Sutton after he checked in?"

"Yes, I saw them after they came back from dinner."

"About what time was that?"

"I'm not sure," Pete said, looking up at the ceiling. "Eight thirty, maybe nine."

"Did you see him after that, that night?"

"No, I didn't," Pete said. "Um, he and his wife retired for the night."

"Did he call you at all after that?"

"No. I didn't hear from him the rest of the night. I did see him the next morning."

"Mister Kelly," the prosecutor said. "Paul Sutton testified to leaving around 1:15 AM in the morning. Now if you never left your post, how come you didn't see him?"

Pete Kelly's eternal smile slowly turned into a frown as he appeared stunned. "Um, I'm not sure."

"Isn't there a way to exit their suite without going by the front desk?"

"Um yeah, I guess there is. You could go out the back alley and out to the parking lot. But, people usually go out by da front desk."

"So, it would have been possible for Paul Sutton to leave your resort out the back alley earlier that night and drive down to Kings City and back without you seeing him?"

"I suppose," Pete said grudgingly. "But, I don't believe that for a second. He came here to get away from Kings City and enjoy his anniversary."

"Yes, that's what he told you," the prosecutor said. "Would your resort deliver wine directly to the room of someone staying at your resort?"

"Why, yes, if they asked."

"One more question, Mister Kelly. Is the quality of the wine pretty good at your resort?"

Pete Kelly laughed, before saying, "I'd like to think so."

The prosecuting attorney said that he no further questions.

The defense attorney stood up behind the desk and asked, "Does your resort carry Fetzer Merlot?"

"No, we don't," Pete replied, shaking his head. The defense attorney thanked Pete and said that she had no further questions.

The defense attorney recalled Officer James Cummings. I remembered he was the officer who gave Paul Sutton a ticket a few hours after the murder. As he approached the stand, he again walked in full uniform. He sat up straight in his chair with a serious expression on his face.

"Officer Cummings. For our recollection, who do you work for?"

"Stanislaus Police Force."

"Yes, Stanislaus," the defense attorney said slowly. "Do you know where Bill's Liquor store is?"

"Yes, I do."

The defense attorney grabbed People's Exhibit 7. "Where is it located in relation to the spot where you gave Paul Sutton this ticket?"

"About four blocks east on Main Street."

"I see. So, if Paul visited Bill's Liquor store, he would have to drive right by the Exxon station to get back to Highway 5. Isn't that correct?"

"Yes, that's right."

"The truth is you have no evidence, no proof that Paul Sutton had just driven from Kings City which is what the prosecution alleges. Do you?"

"No, I don't."

"Of course you don't," the defense attorney said. "And you have no reason to doubt the defendant's statement that he just came from Bill's Liquors before stopping at the Exxon station on his way back to Highway 4?"

"No, I don't," Officer Cummings said, stressing the word "I". The defense attorney appeared satisfied as she stated that she had no further questions.

From his chair, the prosecutor said, "We have no questions for this witness, your honor."

The defense recalled Sallie Anderson, who was Gary Bender's fiancée. She appeared as frightened and pale as the last time.

Eric J. Lee

"Yesterday, you testified that you and Gary Bender were going to buy a home near the beach and take a cruise to Europe."

"That's correct."

"Ms. Anderson, what do you do for a living?"

"I'm a secretary."

"I'm a little confused," the defense attorney said pausing. "You work as a secretary. Gary was a partner in Buckley Liquors that Mister Buckley said was doing poorly. So, how could you two afford a cruise to Europe, and a beach home?"

A blank stare came across Ms. Anderson. "I don't know. Gary just said he was going to take care of everything."

"Do you think it is possible that Gary was lying to you?"

"No," Ms. Anderson said, shaking her head for emphasis. "Gary was an honest man. He'd never lie to me."

"Honest? He took illegal bribes from underage teenagers."

"Objection," the prosecutor said. "Argumentative."

The defense attorney said, "This witness said he was honest. I'm pointing out the inconsistencies among the prosecution's witnesses."

The judge's face forehead wrinkled before he said, "Overruled, but stick to questioning the witness."

"I'm sorry, your honor," the defense attorney said before turning back to the witness. "Ms. Anderson, did you know Gary Bender took bribes from teenagers who wanted to buy beer?"

"No, I didn't. And I don't believe that he did."

"No further questions," the defense attorney said before the prosecutor asked Ms. Anderson a few meaningless questions.

The defense then recalled Jason Buckley to the stand. Buckley, again dressed in a suit, sat down, apparently calm and composed. The defense attorney began, "The first time you testified you said that your profits were slim. Just how small were your profits last year?"

Buckley looked up at the ceiling, pausing to think. "Well, net we've averaged about $24,000 per store."

"And since Gary is only involved with one store and has a 50% interest in that store, he'd make about $12,000 a year. Is that correct?"

"About," Buckley said squirming in his seat. "He also made about $22,000 in salary working there."

"Did Gary work at any other place besides Buckley Liquors?"

"Not that I know of."

"According to his fiancée, Gary bought an engagement ring, planned to take a European cruise and to buy a beachfront home. How could he do this if his sole source of income, Buckley Liquors, was doing as poorly as you claim?"

The prosecutor objected based on lack of foundation, but the judge overruled the objection after only few seconds of thought. The judge instructed Buckley to answer the question, if he knew the answer. "I don't know," Buckley said, shrugging his shoulders.

The defense attorney decided to switch gears. "Mister Buckley, did you know that Gary Bender took illegal bribes from underage teenagers trying to buy alcohol?"

Buckley's forehead wrinkled as he stared menacingly at the defense attorney. "That's preposterous."

"Oh, we have evidence and testimony that Gary took a bribe. So, you're saying you didn't know he did this?"

"Absolutely not."

"One more question Mister Buckley. Gary Bender's 50% partnership interest in the store, which you claim isn't worth very much, did it all revert to you after his death?" Buckley's face turned red as he glared at the defense attorney.

"Objection, your honor," the prosecutor said. "Irrelevant. Paul Sutton, not Jason Buckley, is on trial here."

"Sustained," the judge said in agreement before warning the defense attorney.

"All right. No further questions of this witness."

The prosecutor briskly walked up to Buckley and asked, "Isn't it true that one of the reasons that your profits are so slim is because you have been robbed?"

"Yes, that's true," Buckley replied. "In addition to the robbery in question, we were robbed about nine months before."

"And that prompted you to get a video security system?"

"Well, we already had one camera. We really didn't want to spend a lot more money. So, Gary installed a cheaper camera himself. He had a knack for those things."

"That was the hidden camera, the camera we viewed the murder from?"

"Yeah," Buckley responded. "The murderer just destroyed the first camera. I'm just glad Gary installed the other camera."

"No further questions," the prosecutor said before walking back to his seat.

The defense stood up and said she had no further questions for Buckley and that the defense rested. It was 4:20 so the judge adjourned the court informing us that tomorrow morning we would begin with closing arguments and then the jury would be sent into deliberation.

I walked out of the courtroom with a strange feeling. I had now heard all of the evidence and I now had to decide the fate of a man. As I made my trek to my car, a white sedan pulled up to the sidewalk and playfully honked. It was Barbara. Boy, she can be annoying. She'll be a tough one to deal with in deliberations. She waved and I had to admit I was jealous when I noticed her car was so new she had yet to get license plates.

My alarm gave me a rude awakening at 7:15 on Thursday morning, January 21st. Today was going to be a big day. After the lawyer's closing arguments, the jury would finally get to deliberate. Frankly, I was dying to talk about the case. I had kept an open mind and was still unsure whether the defendant was guilty, but I was anxious to find out what others thought. I got dressed, grabbed a cup of coffee and headed to the courthouse. I arrived a couple of minutes early. It was a little chilly outside, intensified by a noticeable windy breeze. Richard, again dressed formally in slacks and vest, talked on a pay phone just outside the court building. With a scarf around her neck, Catherine was busy knitting again, and she was making considerable progress. Next to Catherine was the meticulous Nancy, who was engrossed in a novel. I'm almost positive that she began the novel just a couple of days ago, but as I approached I could tell she was more than halfway through.

Not wanting to disturb either of those two, I sat down on another bench next to David who was apparently having a conversation with Howard. However, it quickly became apparent that David was doing all of the talking.

The two said hello to me and I said, "You know, I'll find out soon enough when we go into deliberations, but I don't think I really know all the jurors."

"I bet we know all of them between the three of us," David said, making a game of it.

I looked around and saw a woman and a man joking as if they had known each other for years. I vaguely remember seeing them earlier in the week, but I don't think I was ever introduced. "Do you know those two over there?" I asked, pointing to the couple.

"Yeah," David said. "That's uh, Max and, uh, Victoria."

"Okay that's two," I said, beginning to count. "There's us three- that's five. There's Jonathan and Laura. That's seven."

"Those two over there," David said, pointing to Catherine and Nancy. "That's nine."

"Well, there's Richard on the phone over there," I said. "And how could we forget Barbara."

"That's only eleven. Who is the twelfth?" David asked.

Amazingly, Howard spoke. "Aye, didn't name Karen. Sits next to me in court."

I nodded impressed that we could name everyone in the jury. Just then, the bailiff came outside and called all of us into the courtroom. Everyone, the judge, attorneys, and defendant were waiting for us.

As we settled down, the judge addressed us. "As you can see, one of you is missing." I looked around and realized that there was an empty chair. I quickly tried to figure out who was missing. It was Barbara.

"Juror #8 will not be able to make it for at least a couple of hours. We could wait for her to arrive or choose an alternate." The judge looked down at the defense attorney.

"The defense moves to continue with no further delays, and thus would like to choose an alternate juror."

The judge turned to the prosecutor. "The people agree. In the interest of time, we should select an alternate for juror #8."

"All right," the judge said, looking down. "The first alternate is Ms. Lucy Cole. Ms. Cole?"

A small, slender woman awkwardly raised her hand and said, "Here."

"Please take the open seat in the jury box," the judge said. After Lucy changed seats, the judge informed us that we would first hear closing arguments, then he would give us instructions and finally we would go into deliberations.

The judge reminded us that closing arguments are not evidence, merely summations by the lawyers. The judge nodded to the prosecutor, who rose and walked over to us. "Ladies and gentlemen of the jury, I'm going to talk to you for a few moments, and then the defense will get an opportunity, and I will again get a chance to make my final points. In my second discussion, I'd like to talk about the defendant's flawed alibi. But now, I'd like to review the overwhelming evidence against the defendant. When you go back to that juror room and sort through the evidence, you will be left with a set of clear, proven facts."

The prosecutor paused. I'm not sure for effect or if he just wanted to organize his thoughts. "Paul Sutton is the husband of a successful senator. But, for a couple in their position, they were struggling economically. Financial records showed the facts. Their house and car were almost fully mortgaged. And their savings were meager. So…fact….Paul Sutton was in need of money."

The prosecutor slowly paced back and forth in front of us. "Despite all of the smoke the defense will try to cloud the issue, Gary Bender knew Paul Sutton. Let me repeat that. Gary Bender knew Paul Sutton. Ms. Anderson, Gary's fiancée, testified to you that Gary said he knew the senator. And remember, Buckley Liquors proximity to Kings City High School. Conveniently located, Paul admitted he had been there on many occasions. And finally, and most importantly, there were fourteen, repeat, fourteen phone calls from Gary Bender's phone line to Paul Sutton's unlisted number in the last year. As you will see when you investigate the phone bill in your deliberations, one call lasted thirty-six minutes. Now folks, when was the last time you talked on the phone to someone you didn't know for thirty-six minutes?"

The prosecutor put his hands on the railing in front of the jury. "So, fact, Paul did know Gary Bender. And fact, Paul was in desperate need of money. It really isn't important what motive Paul Sutton had for robbing and killing Gary Bender. It's only important that you realize that he did have a motive! Of course, you need more than a motive to prove murder. You

Eric J. Lee

need evidence. And boy do we have it stacked up against Paul Sutton. Two different people saw him drive up to Buckley Liquors, get out of his Porsche 914 and enter the store. Now, we all saw the brutal murder on the videotape and both witnesses could accurately testify the defendant was wearing a mask and a Chicago Bulls jacket. This is the same outfit as the man on the videotape.

Now, who are these witnesses? Are they competent? Are they believable? Of course they are. Both were in Paul Sutton's classroom day after day. Obviously, they know his height, build, and mannerisms and can identify him. Both Alan and Brad gave you unrefuted testimony that they have 20/20 vision. And the two witnesses simply have no reason to lie. Even the defense witness, principal Perry King, admits Alan Clark is an honest, good student. Alan didn't drink that night. His mind was clear. Alan saw Paul Sutton's face when he was in his Porsche 914. A car, by the way, that Alan could easily identify because it was the car that he adored. But, this was not just any Porsche 914, it was Paul Sutton's, identified by the key mark which both witnesses noticed as Paul pulled up to Buckley Liquors. Now, where did Alan and Brad see Paul Sutton? The defense tried to try to cloud the issue by talking about how late it was and arguing it was dark. But, remember, Mister Buckley, the owner of the store, testified to you that he always keeps his parking lots well lit at night."

"Despite Alan's impeccable credentials, the real reason you should believe Alan and Brad is that their testimony is corroborated by other people and evidence. Remember, Mrs. Wells, who normally takes a walk after coming home from a late shift, could identify a red sports car racing from the parking lot of Buckley Liquors that night. Sgt. James Griffin testified that a search of Paul Sutton's home a few days later revealed a Chicago Bulls jacket in Paul Sutton's closet. Not any Chicago Bulls jacket, a jacket with a hanging thread, which an expert

testified matched the one on the videotape. That same expert
testified that Paul Sutton's weight and height fall within the
narrow ranges based on detailed analysis of the video. Now,
ladies and gentlemen, if you objectively look at all of the
evidence, there will be no conclusion you can reach other than
guilty."

The defense attorney then rose and walked over to the jury.
"In our system, the prosecution has the burden of proof. They
have to prove beyond a reasonable doubt that Paul Sutton is
guilty of robbery and murder." The defense attorney paused.
"As anyone who knew him would tell you, and as his boss
Principal Perry King and his brother Shawn Sutton did testify to,
Paul Sutton is a good, decent man, who has never even been
suspected of a crime in his entire life." I glanced at Paul who
was not looking at his attorney, instead staring straight ahead at
the judge with his hands clenched together.

"Let's get something straight. Paul did NOT have any
motive for robbing and killing Gary Bender. He was not in need
of money and he certainly did not know him. As his brother
Shawn told you, Paul grew up in a small one-bedroom house in
a lower-class neighborhood. He didn't rob or kill anyone for
money back then. Now, he's married to a senator, a United
States senator, and drives a Porsche 914. And the prosecution is
trying to get you to believe he would rob and kill someone for
money, $107 mind you. That's preposterous!" The defense
attorney wagged her right index finger at us as she said, "And
another point. Paul did not know Gary Bender. If he knew him,
someone, anyone, would have been called in here to testify that
they knew each other, or at least say they saw them together.
And ladies and gentlemen, if Paul knew Gary, he most certainly
would have called him at some time over the last five years!
No, the fact is that Paul did not know Gary and he wasn't in
need of money." The defense attorney coughed and took a

moment to walk back to take a drink of water which sat on her desk.

She quickly returned, saying, "Paul Sutton is a teacher. A great teacher, according to the school's principal. But, Paul did things by the book." As the defense attorney spoke, she slowly paced back and forth being sure to make eye contact with every juror. "Now what does 'by the book' mean? Well, it means if you are failing a class as Brad Logan was doing, you don't get your grade raised just because you're a football star. Now, both Brad and his close buddy Alan resented Paul Sutton deeply for this. I want you to remember something when you go back into deliberations. I asked one of these boys what emotions he felt toward Paul Sutton and the response was 'I was upset with him'." The defense attorney took a noticeable pause. "Ladies and gentlemen, those are Brad Logan's words, not mine!"

The defense attorney paused again. "The prosecution's entire case is based on these two obviously resentful, biased kids. Now, I'm not saying they made up the entire story. Maybe they did, I don't know. I do know Paul was nowhere near Buckley Liquors at 11:30 on October 15th. Now, when you already have a predisposed anger toward someone, it can cloud your vision. It can make you see something you want to see. And, of course, it makes life, especially for a kid, interesting and exciting when you let your imagination go. With this mindset already entrenched in Alan and Brad, I don't think they could accurately determine who or what they saw at 11:30 at night. I repeat AT NIGHT. It was dark. And they were trying to identify a man wearing a mask from thirty feet away. And don't forget, Brad was drunk. Now how reliable is a drunken boy's vision at 11:30 at night in identifying someone wearing a mask thirty feet away. Sounds ridiculous, doesn't it? But, this is what the prosecution is relying on."

"Throughout this case, I've tried to illustrate the inconsistencies among the prosecution's own witnesses. Jason

Buckley came in here and said that Gary only made, including his share of the profits, about $34,000 last year. But, Sallie Anderson said Gary was going to buy a beachfront home and take a European cruise. And on one hand, Sallie Anderson and Jason Buckley say Gary Bender is a good honest man. But on the other hand, Brad Logan testified that Gary Bender took illegal bribes to buy alcohol from a teenager. These are the prosecution witnesses! What do these inconsistencies prove? Well, at worst, it means that some of the prosecution witnesses are lying. And at best, some of the prosecution witnesses have a distorted view of what really was going on. If you know some of the things the prosecution witnesses are telling you are wrong, you have to question the rest of their testimony."

"Look, I've been around a long time. I've seen a lot of cases, but I've never seen such a sinisterly poor case that has ever gone to trial. The prosecution has not shown any motive. The prosecution has not shown any past history showing the defendant would be capable of such a brutal, senseless crime. The prosecution has not shown any physical evidence…no hair fibers, no fingerprints, no murder weapon, no mask, nothing."

The defense attorney slowly walked away. I thought she was through, but she then turned around and said, "So, the prosecution's case simply was not enough to prove Paul Sutton is guilty beyond a reasonable doubt. Paul never had to take the stand. The defense never had to say anything because the prosecution did not prove their case. However, Paul did take the stand. He explained how at 11:30 he was over 100 miles away with his wife, happily celebrating his anniversary. That same day, you heard from his wife, a highly respected public official, telling you she was with him at 11:30, substantiating Paul's alibi. You heard from Pete Kelly, who said Paul did make the reservation and testified that he saw him at his resort that night in Stanislaus, a city 100 miles away from Buckley Liquors."

The defense attorney paused momentarily. "I think one of the most frustrating aspects of this case is the profile of the victim, Gary Bender. We don't know much about him. We do know that he has a low moral standard. He sold beer to kids. Furthermore, he bribed the kids for it. What else do we know?" the defense attorney said, looking up at the courtroom ceiling. "He said he had a lot more money than he could ever make working honestly at Buckley Liquors. What does this mean? Maybe he's the type of guy who steals from his business partner or lies to his fiancée. Here is the point ladies and gentlemen of the jury: Gary Bender's questionable morals and suspect financial success could cause a whole host of people to be angry enough to want to kill him. Please remember that."

The defense attorney stopped pacing and put her hands on the railing. "Let me end with this. What has the prosecution proven that shows Paul Sutton is the one who is guilty?" The defense attorney held up both hands balled up in a fist. As she spoke, she counted with her fingers, "No motive, no negative past history, no hair fibers, no fingerprints, no murder weapon, no mask, no blood evidence, and no consistency in the testimony of witnesses." The defense paused to look at her eight fingers raised in the air. "Ladies and gentlemen, it is clear that Paul Sutton is not guilty. It is obvious that Paul is not guilty beyond a reasonable doubt. Please don't send an innocent man to jail and possibly to his death. Please." The defense attorney slowly walked back to her seat.

The prosecuting attorney walked up to the jury with a serious look on his face. "Let's talk about Paul Sutton's alibi. Ladies and gentleman, it's inconsistent, illogical and hopelessly 'cooked up'. Paul says, upon arriving in Stanislaus, he and his wife checked in, and then had dinner and went for a walk. The hotel manager testified that he saw the two come back around 8:30, nine o'clock. Now, Paul expects you to believe he stayed in his room for about five hours before, poof, he gets the idea he

wants a special brand of wine. Never mind that it's one thirty in
the morning. Never mind he's in an unfamiliar city. Never
mind that it's freezing cold outside, remember it was thirty
degrees. Never mind that he will have to leave his wife on a
night that was supposed to be romantic." As the prosecutor
rattled through his points, his voice started to get louder. "And
never mind the fact that the resort could have delivered perfectly
good wine right to his room! No, despite all of this, Paul Sutton
wants you to believe that he left his warm room and lovely wife
to search for a specific type of wine at 1:30 in the morning in a
cold, unfamiliar city!"

The prosecutor smiled and slightly shook his head. "Now,
why would Paul make up this ridiculous story about getting
wine? Well, he needed some excuse for being out late on
October 15th because it is in police records that he ran a red
light at 1:55 that night. And he certainly doesn't want to tell you
the truth- that he got that ticket when he was returning to
Stanislaus from Kings City after he robbed and murdered Gary
Bender."

The prosecutor turned and pointed to the defendant and said,
"That man is a cold-blooded killer. He planned to use this trip
as an alibi." The prosecutor slowly dropped his arm and turned
back toward the jury. "I want to talk to you about facts.
Remember, no defense witness other than the defendant's own
wife can account for Paul Sutton's whereabouts from 9:00 P.M.
to 1:55 AM. I repeat, no one other than his wife! So, sometime
between 9:00 P.M. and 10:00 P.M., Paul left the resort out of the
back exit, repeat back exit, so that Pete Kelly wouldn't see him.
This allowed Paul plenty of time to drive down to Kings City by
11:30 P.M. At exactly 11:33 P.M., he was spotted by two eye-
witnesses entering Buckley Liquors where he robbed and
murdered Gary Bender. He was spotted by another eye-witness,
Mrs. Wells, speeding away from Buckley Liquors. He sped
back to Stanislaus where he got a traffic ticket running a red

light at 1:55 A.M., which is documented in police records. These are the facts. This is the timeline."

The prosecutor leaned on the railing in front of the jury as if to make one final connection with us. "Ladies and gentlemen of the jury, the defense has done its best to cloud these facts with things that are irrelevant. This case isn't about politics. It's not about football. It's definitely not about the victim's own personal life. And it's not about what kind of teacher Paul Sutton is. You can't reach your decision based on pity or compassion. Now, if you decide this case strictly on the evidence, the only just verdict would be to find the defendant guilty on both counts."

The prosecutor then reached into his pocket as he pulled out a folded sheet of paper. "Ladies and gentlemen, Sallie Anderson gave this to me. It's a wedding invitation. Moments ago, the defense said that you do not know much about the victim Gary Bender. This invitation is all you need to know." The prosecutor slowly opened up the invitation and said, "The invitation announces the wedding of Mr. Gary Bender and Ms. Sallie Anderson. It's supposed to happen in four weeks. This wedding will not happen. The invitation never got sent." The prosecutor paused a moment before walking back to his seat. The trial was over. All of the testimony had been heard, evidence presented, and arguments made. It was time for us to make our decision.

I quickly found out that we weren't going to deliberate immediately. First, we had to listen to the judge read page after page. He gave the statutory definitions of evidence and burden of proof. He explained the exact law that constitutes robbery and first-degree murder. Most of the material was common sense, and all of it was boring. I looked at my watch, which read 9:55 AM as I let my mind wander. Even Nancy seemed a bit uninterested, not taking notes, while I'm sure David actually closed his eyes. There were two important things that the judge said during his long speech. First, to find the defendant guilty, we had to believe it so beyond a reasonable doubt. Second, if the prosecution and the defense provide different versions of particular events AND we believe both versions are reasonable and believable, then we must accept the defense's version.

Finally, the judge formally dismissed us to deliberate. We were escorted out of the courtroom by the bailiff and led upstairs to a juror room. As I entered the dreary room, I was nonetheless excited. I finally had the opportunity to be an active participant in this case as opposed to a mere observer.

The room was nothing special. In the center of the room was a large wooden, rectangular table. There were twelve medium-sized, cushioned chairs around the table with two at each end and four along each of the long sides. The room's four walls had no pictures and only a small window. Apparently, they did not want anything to distract us.

The twelve of us walked in and we all chose a chair. I took a seat on the long side at a corner by the window. David had followed me and sat adjacent to me.

We all looked at the bailiff, hoping he'd give us some guidance. He did. The bailiff took the toothpick out of his mouth and put his hands on his hips. "My name is John. I'm going to be your connection to the outside world. If you need anything, want to ask the judge a question, or need to leave to take a break or go to lunch, you buzz me on this intercom and I'll come up as soon as I can."

"You sayin' we're locked in here?" Howard blurted out.

"I suppose you can say that," John replied. He opened a door in the short hallway that led to our table. "Restrooms are in here. So you don't have to call me for that. Now, the first thing you all need to do is elect a foreperson. Someone to write all inquiries to the court, be your representative, and of course, read the verdict. Now I prefer not to be in here while you all are discussing juror business. So, I'll be right outside."

After John left, we stared at each other awkwardly for a couple of moments before Laura asked, "Well, does anyone want to be foreperson?"

A couple of seconds passed before Nancy and I simultaneously said, "I'll do it," which prompted a slight laugh from several jurors.

I deferred to Nancy, who quickly accepted her new position. "I think we should take a break," Nancy said. "We haven't had one yet."

"Must we? I was hoping we would be able to speed through this as fast as possible," Richard said as he made circular motions with his right hand.

"We'll make it a short one," Nancy said, already trying to exert her authority. "Let's say ten minutes."

Everyone headed out. John had brought up all the exhibits and locked the door behind us. He told us that none of our notes or exhibits would be allowed outside the juror room. I headed outside. Dark clouds began to gather overhead, but the fresh, cold air was still a welcomed change from inside the stuffy courtroom. Once outside, I decided to introduce myself to Max and Victoria. A pilot for an overnight delivery service, Victoria said her experience in the Air Force taught her about making tough decisions.

It turns out military service was something Victoria and Max had in common. After high school, Max had served in the Army for six years. He struck me as someone who liked to appear tough. I guessed he would be a loud voice during deliberations.

Once our ten-minute break was up, everyone reassembled outside the juror room. John let us all in and we took our seats. The twelve of us looked around, not knowing exactly where to begin.

Nancy, looking prim and proper, put on her reading glasses and opened her notepad, which must have been full. "Why don't we go around the room and say our first names? I don't think everyone knows everyone else. I'm Nancy."

Nancy turned to her left and looked at Laura who was also at the end of the table. It continued clockwise, with Max, Victoria, David, and me on one side. At the other end and to my immediate left was Jonathan and Karen and on the other side, sat Richard, Howard, Lucy and Catherine. "Now, how should we start?" Nancy asked openly.

"Let's take a vote," David said.

"A vote?" Victoria said. "We haven't discussed anything yet."

"I know," David said. "It'll be like a preliminary vote. Just to see how people feel before we discuss it."

"I don't know if that's such a good idea," I said. I had hoped we could discuss all the evidence before coming to conclusions.

"Well," David said. "Can we at least take a vote on whether we can take a vote?"

"Look," Nancy said, exerting control. "Let's take a quick vote. But, if you have no strong feelings one way or the other because you would like to discuss it first, vote undecided." Everyone thought this was a good compromise. "All those who believe the defendant is guilty on the two counts- raise your hand." Max and David's hands immediately shot up and Howard's slowly followed. "Not guilty?" Nancy asked, causing Richard, Laura, and Catherine to each raise their hand. The rest of us raised our hand for undecided, perhaps indicating our protest against the premature vote.

At Victoria's suggestion, we read the instructions on what constitutes robbery and first-degree murder. It was mostly common sense, so we came to a somewhat obvious conclusion. It would be virtually impossible to find Paul Sutton guilty of only one count. Basically, if we believe he was the man on that videotape, then he's guilty on both counts. And if we don't believe he was the one on the videotape, he was not guilty on either count.

We began to explore the exhibits individually. I picked up People's Exhibit 1. It was a small photograph of the victim, Gary Bender. He was a very handsome man, probably in his mid 30s. He was in the prime of his life. "What a shame. Why would anyone want to kill you?" I thought as I stared at the picture.

"See something special," David said, which startled me.

"No," I said as I slowly put the picture down. "Nothing special." David shrugged, and I went over to review the exhibits that interested me most, Gary Bender's and Paul Sutton's phone bills.

"We're wasting time here," Richard said, addressing all of us. "We've seen these exhibits. Besides, we can discuss the exhibits when they're relevant. I suggest that we list evidence against the defendant. We can then make our own fact-based judgments. We could be out of here by the end of the day."

"Aye," Howard said. He gestured toward Richard. "I agree with him. Soona we can get out of here, the better."

Nancy frowned. "Fine. Let's all take our seats." Everyone slowly took their original seats before Nancy asked, "What evidence do we have against Paul Sutton, indicating that he robbed and killed Gary Bender?"

"Now, we're talking," David said, rubbing his hands together. "Well, there's Alan and Brad's testimony."

Richard shook his head. "I don't put too much weight in their testimony. They were biased, drunk, and their vision couldn't have been too accurate at night."

"Don't put too much weight in their testimony?" Max asked in a surprised tone. "That's eye-witness testimony. You sayin' they're makin' all this up."

"Don't put words in my mouth," Richard said. "All I'm saying is there are a lot of problems with their testimony. I have some real doubts that they in fact saw what they say they saw."

I was listening closely to Max and Richard. I didn't need that straw poll earlier to know where Max and Richard stood. "I think it's important to separate Alan and Brad," I said, finally speaking up. "I think they have different levels of credibility. And I think they saw different things."

"That's right. Correct me if I'm wrong," Laura said, looking down at her notepad. "But, Brad admitted that he never saw Paul's face."

"But, he saw the key mark on the car," Howard said. "Means he saw Paul's car."

Richard snickered. "I don't trust Brad any farther than I can throw him. He's a punk. He's the one who keyed the car in the first place!"

"That's what bothers me," I said, scratching my head. "If Brad is such a dishonest punk, why didn't he just lie in court and say he didn't key the car? I mean why does he all of a sudden tell the truth?"

"Look, I'm the youngest person on this jury," Jonathan said. "So, I've been in high school more recently than all of you. Do you know how big it is to be a star football player in high school? You're instantly popular. You get all of the girls. All of the guys want to be your friend. It's your ticket to a college scholarship and maybe even the pros."

"What's your point?" Max asked.

"My point is…" Jonathan said slowly. "In Brad's mind, Paul took all of that away from him. That principal's testimony proves how upset Brad was. Here's the bottom line. I don't trust Brad." Jonathan shook his head slightly before adding, "Not at all."

Catherine, who brought her knitting materials into the juror room, stopped her work for a moment and said, "Plus, let's not forget Brad was drunk."

"Actually, we don't really know if he was drunk," David said. "All we know is he had some beers earlier."

"Oh come on," Richard said. "The boy was drunk. He was making a beer run."

"Okay," Nancy said, trying to keep some order. "Let's review what we have on Brad. He saw Paul's car drive up to Buckley Liquors that night. And mitigating factors are that Brad is biased against the defendant, he was drunk, and it was dark." Nancy asked if anyone wanted to talk further about Brad. When no one responded, we moved over to Alan.

"Well, Alan saw the defendant's face," David said.

"Now that doesn't make any sense," Richard said. "Now, if I were going to rob a store, I wouldn't put on my mask at the scene of the crime."

"Aye, don't think Paul saw them boys," Howard said.

"Here's the bottom line on the whole case," Max said. "Alan is not biased. Alan was not drunk. His eyesight is perfect. He testified to clearly seeing the defendant. Now, how can you refute that?"

I shared my thoughts with the group. "I really believe Alan thought he saw Paul that night. However, it was dark and he had to make a split-second decision on identification. He could have just made an honest mistake."

Max and Howard shook their heads in disagreement. At this point, it was clear the only thing we all could agree on was to take a break for lunch. We told the bailiff that we wished to view the videotape first thing after lunch. Not the most pleasant way to digest your lunch, but so be it.

After lunch, both attorneys were present for the viewing of the videotape. It was the third time it was played for us. Even up close, there was no way I could tell if that was Paul Sutton.

When the videotape ended, the bailiff and the two attorneys left. "Did anyone notice the murderer lean over Gary after killing him? Now why was that?" Laura asked.

"He was probably just checking to see if Gary had a wallet," Victoria offered. "To see if any money was in there."

I shook my head. "I don't think so. A robber checks a dead body for chump change, but doesn't look under the cash drawer in the register." I tapped my index finger on the table. "No, I believe whoever killed Gary, did it for some reason other than money."

There was an awkward silence in the jury room, before Karen said, "Maybe he was checking to see if he was dead."

"Doubt that too," I said. "If you're only interested in money, you wouldn't waste any time after you shoot someone. You'd get out of there."

"Can we get back to listing evidence against the defendant?" Richard asked.

"Well, there's the Chicago Bulls jacket they found in his clothes hamper," Victoria said. "With that hanging thread, exactly like the one on the videotape."

"Oh, the Bulls are a popular team, especially in this area," Richard argued. "And the thread, I admit; that's bad. But, it's possible it's a common problem on that type of jacket."

"No, no," David said, shaking his head. "That thread is the smoking gun. It proves it was the defendant's jacket, which pretty much proves it was the defendant."

"Well, I don't think the thread proves it on its own," I said. "But, it *is* strong evidence against the defendant." I looked at Nancy who was feverishly taking notes.

"How about the lady who saw Paul's car leave the parking lot," Victoria said.

"She couldn't even identify the type of car," Catherine said, knitting. "I don't put any validity in her testimony."

"You're right," Nancy said, looking at her notes. "I have down that she could only say it was a red sports car.

"But," Max said, wagging his finger in the air. "That shows Alan and Brad didn't make up the whole story."

"Kind of proves what I've been saying," I said. "Brad and Alan at least thought they saw Paul Sutton."

"Any more evidence against Paul?" Nancy asked, slightly cutting me off.

"There's the phone bills," David said, reaching for the exhibit. "Gary made over fourteen phone calls over the last two years, including one call one week before the murder. Now that proves Paul knew Gary Bender."

"No," I said. "I believe it only means that Gary knew Gloria or Paul, or maybe both."

"You know, I don't care if Gary and Paul were bosom buddies," Richard said, shifting back in his chair and folding his arms in front of his chest. "How does that prove that he killed Gary?"

"It would prove that Paul misrepresented the facts," Victoria said. "Just like he misrepresented how much money he and Gloria had. He said they were well-off. Heck, I don't call someone whose house is fully mortgaged and can't pay down their car loan well-off."

"Makes you wonder how they squandered all that money," David said. "Senators are paid well."

"I agree with Robert," Laura said, which made me smile. "I think if you look at the videotape closely, that gunman wasn't interested in money. So, I think Paul's financial position is irrelevant." I thought about Laura's statement and I guess that I had to agree.

"Let me review where we are," Nancy said, trying to bring some order back to the deliberations. "Evidence against Paul

Sutton. One, Brad's testimony. He saw Paul's marked car pull up to Buckley Liquors. However, he may be biased, and/or drunk. Also, it was dark. Two, Alan's testimony. He actually saw Paul's face and he also recognized the car. However, he may also be biased and it was dark. Three, Mrs. Wells' testimony. She saw a red sports car, which corroborates, to some extent, Alan and Brad's testimony. Four, the Chicago Bulls jacket found in Paul's closet with the hanging thread, similar to the one the robber wore. And five, the phone bill which might indicate that Paul knew Gary. Anything else?"

"Don't forget Doctor Baculi," Max commented. "He said that the person on that videotape had similar height and weight as the defendant."

"That doesn't prove that it was him," Catherine said.

"What do you mean *prove*?" Max asked Catherine. "It's evidence from an expert."

"It is another factor against him," Nancy said, jotting it down in her notepad.

"I just want to say that there are literally millions of people with similar height, weight and build as Paul Sutton," Richard argued. "Just in this room, Howard over there, and um... sorry what's your name?" Richard asked, pointing to Jonathan.

"Jonathan," the youngest jury member replied.

"Right," Richard said, snapping his fingers. "Just here in this room, Jonathan and Howard have similar height, weight and build as Paul Sutton."

"Plus the Bulls jacket was pretty baggy," Karen added. "Which means the person didn't necessarily have the same build."

"Any more evidence against the defendant?" Nancy asked abruptly.

"Ain't that enough?" Howard said with a groan.

"That's a decision that we'll have to make individually," Nancy responded. She switched gears when no one had anything else to add against the defendant. "Now, in juror instructions, it clearly states that if you have two reasonable and believable stories, you must find for the defendant."

Victoria said, "In other words, even if you believe everything that the prosecution has said, if you find Paul's alibi believable and reasonable, we must find for the defendant."

"Well, let's talk about Paul's alibi," Nancy said, opening the floor for discussion.

"I, for one, don't buy it," David argued. "Who goes out for wine at 1:30 AM when they could have ordered room service?"

"Aye," Howard said. "The man's a liar."

"Don't forget though, Gloria can vouch for his complete alibi," Laura said.

"They're both liars," Howard blurted out.

"I don't understand you two," Richard said, shaking his head at David and Howard. "You two don't believe a distinguished senator of the United States, but you think Brad, an admitted vandal, is telling the truth."

"I don't understand the hoopla," Catherine said, calmly knitting. "The man is a romantic. He wanted to get the same type of wine as he had on his wedding night."

We continued to argue about the validity of Paul's alibi. And after all the arguing, we were left with Gloria's corroboration on one side and the strange timing for a wine run on the other.

"We've talked about the evidence against Paul and we've talked about Paul's alibi," Richard said. "But, I think it's important to talk about the victim. The prosecution has tried to portray Gary Bender as a hardworking, honest man. But, this guy took bribes from teenagers. He lied to his fiancée when he said was going to buy all those things for her. Let's face it. On his income, he couldn't afford that stuff."

"How does that relate to the guilt or innocence of Paul Sutton?" Nancy asked, appearing agitated.

"First of all, it's a misrepresentation by the prosecution," Richard said. "And second, Gary's questionable behavior could have made him a lot of enemies who might have wanted to do him harm."

"We really haven't heard from you," Nancy said, looking at Lucy. "What do you think?"

I had forgotten about her. She had yet to say a word. What a stark contrast from the woman she replaced, Barbara. "I don't know," Lucy said meekly.

"You must have some opinion," Richard prodded. "Some observation?"

"Not really," Lucy responded softly. "Not yet."

"I have something to say," Catherine said, speaking up. "We all saw the murder on the videotape. This was not heat of passion. This was premeditated. For someone to do this, he'd have to be an evil person. Did they ever prove that Paul could be capable of a crime like this?" Catherine paused a few seconds. "No," Catherine said, emphatically answering her own question. "What was proven in court was that he was a school teacher who had no prior record."

"That's an excellent point," Richard said, gesturing toward Catherine. "We can't forget the defendant had no prior record."

Max said under his breath, "Every murderer has a first time."

Before an argument could ensue, Laura suggested we shifted gears and talk about Officer Brian Cummings, who pulled over Paul Sutton in Stanislaus the night of the murder. In that discussion, there was a disagreement about the facts so we had the court reporter come up and read his testimony back to us. It was basically how I remembered it. Paul Sutton was pulled over after running a red light. He had just pulled out of a gas station in Stanislaus at 1:55 AM.

The court reporter left and I saw a few yawns among our group. It had been a long day. It was now 4:50, almost the time we usually go home. "Before we go, let's take a vote," David said with smile. "I'd like to see how much progress we've made."

Everyone was much more agreeable to David's request for a vote this time. Nancy told everyone that this vote was just to see where we were and an undecided vote could be cast if you did not have a feeling one way or the other." Nancy paused before saying, "All those for guilty." David, Max and Howard again raised their hand, but this time, Victoria and Karen joined them. "All those for not guilty?" Nancy asked, causing Laura, Richard, Catherine and now Jonathan to raise his hand. So, it was little surprise that Nancy, the quiet Lucy and I were the ones who voted undecided.

"So, that's a 5-4-3 split for guilty, not guilty and undecided," Nancy said, taking off her glasses to rub her eyes.

"It looks like it's going to be hard for us to be unanimous," Laura said with a sigh.

What an experience. My head ached. I had talked for over six hours with strangers. And we really hadn't accomplished much more than a 5-4 split vote. I looked around the table. Others appeared tired as well. Richard exhaled audibly as he sat back in his chair. Jonathan got up to stretch while David massaged his temples.

"Look," Nancy said, looking fatigued. "It's been a long day. I say we quit for the day and we'll resume tomorrow morning at eight thirty."

There seemed to be complete agreement until Richard said, "Before we leave, I have something for you all to think about tonight. The prosecution would like us to believe that Paul Sutton robbed Buckley Liquors at 11:33 PM, right?" We all nodded our heads in agreement, not understanding where Richard was going with this. "And after robbing the store, he headed back to Stanislaus and his alibi. But, he got caught running a red light presumably because he was in a hurry."

"What's your point?" Victoria asked.

Richard smiled. "Paul received the ticket at 1:55 AM. Now, I know how long that drive takes. And they testified to it in court. Without traffic, it would take an hour and a half, at most. That would put him back in Stanislaus at 1:05 AM. The prosecution's timing is off by fifty minutes!"

All of us were momentarily stunned. It appeared that Richard had come up with an excellent point. David broke the silence, "Maybe he stopped somewhere."

"Where?" Richard asked. "It was past midnight! And why? If he did shoot and rob Gary, he would want to get back to Stanislaus and his alibi as soon as possible." The room fell silent. Richard had made his point and we decided to call it a day.

That night, as I lay back in my lounge chair, I had so much on my mind. I still believed Alan and Brad *thought* they saw Paul that night. I had an intriguing question in my mind. If they didn't see Paul, who did they see?

I was sure of one thing: Whoever was on that videotape wanted Gary dead and cared very little about how much money he'd receive. Yet, why was everyone apparently misrepresenting how much money they had? Paul said he was well off, but he really wasn't. And Gary lied, or at least, greatly exaggerated to Sallie how much money he had.

If I find Paul not guilty, how do I come to grips with what seems like a silly alibi for why he was out late that night?

If I vote guilty, I want to be sure. And Richard's observation at the end of the day only made me more doubtful. Why did it take him so long to get back to Stanislaus? I couldn't stomach the thought of sending an innocent man to his death.

Many thoughts went around and around in my mind. I ended up where I began, with the intriguing question. If Paul is not guilty, who is? This was silly because as jurors, we're not trying to figure out who committed the crime. We are only trying to determine if Paul is guilty. But, as a private eye, I still wondered. I wondered whether Paul was just covering up for his high-profile, influential wife, who may have been the one driving his car to Buckley Liquors that night. I wondered whether Shawn Sutton, who certainly looked like his brother Paul, could have any reason to kill Gary. I wondered just how much Sallie Anderson loved Gary and how badly she wanted to get her hands on the money he told her he had. And I wondered about Jason Buckley and how much he wanted Gary out of the partnership that was supposedly doing poorly. And finally, I wondered about the two high school kids, Alan and Brad, and whether they would ever try to frame a man who Brad intensely hated. And on that final thought, I fell asleep.

As I got up the next morning, I could feel it. No, not just the deep ache in my back from sleeping on the lounge chair, it was the feeling that today would be the day we, as jurors, reached a consensus. It was Friday morning and I didn't want this case to go over the weekend.

As I drove down the long two-lane highway to get to the courthouse, I realized that I was very low on gas. I looked at my watch. It was getting late. I decided that I could make it to the courthouse, but I would need to get gas either at lunch or on the way home. As it turned out, I arrived at the courthouse right on time. Since we didn't have to wait for the judge or the attorneys, I figured that we'd start on time. Unfortunately, that was not the case.

After waiting outside of the juror room for fifteen minutes, John came up to us and announced, "Sorry about the hold-up folks. But, you all can't go into deliberations without your foreperson." My quick count did reveal we were one short. John added, "She called in. She was having car problems, but she believes she will be able to get here in about forty minutes."

I could hear Max and Richard groan out loud, but it was Howard who spoke up. "What weze suppose ta do for forty minutes?"

"Well, you're free to go outside," John said. "Just be sure to be back here in forty minutes."

Everyone headed back downstairs, while I stayed to ask John a question. "I know you said Nancy would be here in forty minutes. But, what if she got seriously ill, or into a serious accident or even died?"

"Mistrial," John replied. "All of the alternates were sent home after the trial. So, as soon as you all went into deliberations, it was going to be you twelve coming up with a verdict."

"Exactly what happens in a mistrial?" I asked.

"Same as if you all are hung," John said. "The entire case has to be tried over again with a new jury, but of course, that is if the prosecution wants to do it all over again."

"Why wouldn't they?"

John chuckled. "Well, trials are expensive. The prosecution better believe they have an excellent chance of winning. Otherwise, they'd be better off dropping the case." John glanced at his watch before looking back at me. "Look, just make sure your car is running okay. Two car problems in one jury is enough for me." John started down the hallway.

"Two?" I said, running to catch up with him. "What do you mean two? Who else had car problems besides Nancy?"

"Barbara Hendricks did. You remember her. That's why we had to pick an alternate."

"Oh," I said, not realizing that was why Barbara couldn't make it to court that day. John said he had some court business to attend to so I let him go.

About forty-five minutes later, Nancy arrived and we all took our seats in the juror room. Richard was the first to speak. "I'd be interested in hearing from the three people who are still

Eric J. Lee

undecided. I'd like to know what else they would need to know or hear discussed before they can come to a conclusion."

The question was obviously directed at Lucy, Nancy and me. "Well," I said, speaking up first. "I really think that Pete Kelly's testimony is critical to this case."

"Mister Kelly's testimony?" Laura said surprised. "Why?"

"His ability to corroborate Paul's story is key," I argued. "I know his wife can. But, she's his wife. I would like to hear Pete Kelly's testimony again."

Everyone agreed to get the court reporter up here so we could listen to Pete's testimony again. John told us to expect the court reporter to arrive in half an hour, around 10:15.

"How about you, Nancy?" Richard asked. "What's it going to take to get you to come to a decision?"

"Look, here's where I stand," Nancy said. "There's a lot of evidence against the defendant, no question about it. I'd like to vote guilty, I really would. But, I can't until I can get rid of this unnerving thought."

"What thought is that?" David asked with wrinkled forehead.

"That Paul is being framed." Nancy's statement hit everyone like a blow to the stomach. We were all momentarily speechless, not knowing how to respond. Paul being framed was something I imagine we all had thought about at some point, but wouldn't dare say for fear of looking crazy."

Max broke the silence. "Framed?" Max said with a look of disbelief.

"Please, let me finish," Nancy said, holding her right hand up. "Just keep an open mind. Now, suppose someone knew Paul would be on this trip. That person gets a hold of his Chicago Bulls jacket. Gets a similar Porsche 914 and keys it so it looks exactly like the defendant's car. Wanting to look like the defendant, this person uses the baggy jacket and specific heeled shoes, giving him similar height and weight. I'm voting

110

undecided now, but if I can't get this thought out of my mind, I'm going to vote not guilty."

"Let me get this straight," Max said, resting his right elbow on the table and massaging his forehead. "You are basing your vote on some half-cocked idea he was framed."

"Don't trivialize my position," Nancy said, pointing at Max. "It's fact based. Think about it. The person has Paul's height and Paul's weight. It looks like he has Paul's jacket. It looks like he has Paul's car. But, who's to say it was actually Paul and not someone posing as him?"

"Actually, Alan did," I said, answering Nancy's rhetorical question.

"Two options would explain that," Nancy said, seemingly prepared for my comment. "First, it was dark. Alan had to make a decision in 3 seconds. He was scared and possibly drunk. It is very reasonable to think that since he was convinced he saw Paul's car, he assumed it was Paul."

"What's the other option?" David asked.

"The other option is a bit wilder," Nancy conceded. "But, it's very simple. Alan is the one trying to frame Paul."

Nancy had silenced the room again. Many of us were pondering the validity of Nancy's remarks. It was clear by Max and Howard's expressions that they weren't about to give it a second's thought.

Max seemed to make a calculated decision not to argue with Nancy, instead changing the focus of the conversation. "Okay, I'd like to hear from those voting not guilty. Can you give me a likely scenario for how Gary died if it wasn't Paul, given the evidence?"

"I certainly can," Richard said jumping in. "Buckley said they had been robbed in the past. So another robber driving a red sports car hits the store and kills Gary. It was dark. So, Alan and Brad let their imagination get away with them and,

Eric J. Lee

with deep hatred against Paul, it easy for them to say that it was Paul. The Wells lady sees the robber leave in a red sports car."

There was a hush over the group as everyone seemed to ponder Richard's scenario. "But, weze decided that the murderer wasn't after money," Howard said, challenging Richard. "So it couldn't have been a robber."

"Maybe you subscribe to Robert's theory," Richard said. "But I don't. Buckley said $107 was stolen. Sounds like the robber was interested in money to me."

More arguments went back and forth. I got the feeling we would never reach a consensus until I figured out how I felt and then I could argue my point. I hoped the testimony of Pete Kelly would help. The court reporter arrived, along with John, to read Pete's testimony. It began to get interesting at this point.

"Question: What do you do at the front desk?"

"Answer: Well, I check folks in and out. Take calls for room service. Take complaint calls. Reservation calls. I might be looking at the books. Not a lot, I suppose."

"Question: On October 15th, did you see Paul Sutton?"

"Answer: Yes, I did. He came up about six o'clock to check in. I remember cuz I had just started working the front desk."

"Question: So, you started your shift around six. How long did you stay at the front desk?"

"Answer: Until two a.m. And it was continuous."

"Question: Now, Mister Kelly. You were at the front desk until 2 AM. Did you see Paul leave his room that night? Say about ten o'clock, the time he would have to leave to get to Kings City by 11:30 PM."

"Answer: No. I never saw Paul leave and I never left my post that night." At this point, defense ended their questioning. The prosecution then began asking Pete Kelly questions. It became interesting when the court reporter read.

112

"Question: Mister Kelly. Did you see Paul Sutton after he checked in?"

"Answer: Yes, I saw them after they came back from dinner."

"Question: About what time was that?"

"Answer: I'm not sure. Eight thirty, maybe nine."

"Question: Did you see him after that, that night?"

"Answer: No, I didn't. He and his wife retired for the night."

"Question: Did he call you at all after that?"

"Answer: No. I didn't hear from him the rest of the night. I did see him the next morning."

"Whoa!" I said, not meaning to say that out loud. The court reporter stopped immediately, staring at me. "Could you repeat the last question and answer please?"

"Question: Did he call you at all after that?"

"Answer: No. I didn't hear from him the rest of the night. I did see him the next morning."

The court reporter finished up Pete's testimony and left. It had taken awhile, but I had finally come to a conclusion. I was thinking it was crucial that Pete corroborate Paul's alibi, but instead he had contradicted it.

"Pete said he took phone calls for room service and was on his shift until two a.m.," I said reviewing. "But, he said he never saw or heard from him after eight thirty. Why didn't he call Pete to see if he had that brand of wine before supposedly going out around 1:15 a.m.?"

There was silence in the juror room. No one responded to my question. I stubbornly waited for an answer. "Maybe he knew Pete's resort did not carry that brand of wine," Richard finally said.

I shook my head. "If he knew they didn't carry the wine and this is so important that he leaves for it at one in the morning, why didn't he buy the wine ahead of time?"

"Maybe he just forgot," Catherine said. "People do forget important things sometimes."

"Ah geze," Howard said, pounding his hand on the table. "Man's guilty. This proves it for sure."

"I'm afraid this is another big inconsistency," Laura said. "I think it's going to make me rethink my decision."

"What about you?" Max asked Jonathan. "You voted not guilty before."

"Nope," Jonathan said, shaking his head. "I'm going to need more."

"Same here," Richard said ardently.

Max rolled his eyes before announcing to the group, "Let's take another vote. See where we stand."

We took another straw poll. The vote came out 8-4 for guilty. Undecided votes switching to guilty were Lucy and myself. Nancy, who was undecided before, actually switched to not guilty. Laura was convinced enough with Pete's testimony that she switched from not guilty to guilty. Only Richard, Jonathan and Catherine stuck to their belief that Paul Sutton was not guilty.

"You voted undecided before," Victoria said, looking at Nancy. "Based on what we have been discussing, how can you switch to not guilty?"

"I voted not guilty because I have a reasonable doubt that Paul was framed and that means I have a reasonable doubt about whether he's guilty."

"Doubts!" Max exclaimed, actually rising from his chair. "I'm so sick and tired of hearing that word, doubt. There are no reasonable doubts in this case." Max walked over and picked up Gary Bender's picture. "This man was murdered. We all saw it on videotape. And we have eyewitness testimony from an honor student. There is no reason to believe Alan, a good kid according to a defense witness, would lie."

Catherine turned in her chair and said to a standing Max, "The doubts come into play because there are reasons to believe that Alan may not have been able to see him it. It was almost midnight."

"Oh, that's bogus," Max said. "Buckley testified that the place was well lit. And again, Alan wouldn't lie. If he had some doubt about what he saw, he would have said so."

"How do you know?" Nancy asked, challenging Max. "You don't know Alan."

"Of course I don't," Max shot back. "But, they testified in court that he was an honest honor student who didn't have disciplinary problems. A kid like that doesn't send someone away for life unless he's sure. Period!"

As Max walked back to his seat, Victoria said, "There's more to this case than just Alan's testimony. The key mark, the jacket with a hanging thread, Dr. Baculi's report."

"There's no doubts in this case," Max asserted. "Paul's a killer. Come on people, let's do our job."

Richard took a deep breath. "I've got something to say."

"Please, go ahead," Nancy said as if she wanted to hear from someone other than Max.

"Look, I want to vote guilty based on the prosecution's case," Richard said. "But, I can't. According to the judge's instructions, if the prosecution and the defense both offer reasonable and believable stories about what happened, we must accept the defense's version and find the defendant not guilty. And there's nothing that anyone has said that proves to me that there is anything wrong with the defendant's alibi."

"Give me a break," Max said. "What about that silly story about going out for wine?"

"How do you know he didn't go out for wine?" Richard asked back. "'Cuz, he didn't call for room service as Robert suggested. That's no reason. Maybe he didn't think about room service. Or maybe he thought room service had ended. It was

Eric J. Lee

after one a.m., you know." Richard lay back in his seat, folded his arms, and shook his head. "No, it is possible that he left his resort to get wine. No one has proved to me that it's not possible. And the senator swears it's true."

"She's his wife," Max said. "Of course, she'd lie."

"Maybe she would," Richard said. "But, maybe she wouldn't. Maybe she's just telling the truth. That's possible, isn't it?"

There was a momentary pause. "Anything is possible," Victoria sniped, breaking the silence. "It's possible that this building might collapse in the next five seconds."

"Look," Richard said, noticeably frustrated. "All I'm saying is the defendant's alibi is possible. What hard evidence do we have that the defendant's alibi is not true? Laura, you're voting guilty now. What evidence do you have?" Laura took a deep breath without answering. Apparently, she seemed a little unsure of her new position. Richard didn't wait for her answer saying, "If your answer is 'cuz he went out late and didn't call for room service, I just don't buy that argument."

I heard a few sighs in the room as I could tell fatigue was setting in. "I give up," Max said, throwing his hands up in the air before slumping back in his chair. People were getting tired and frustrated, which was making things more tense and confrontational.

"Look, how about a short break," Nancy said, glancing at her watch. "Let's say about five minutes."

A few people used the break as an opportunity to use the restroom while others studied certain exhibits. I got up to stretch my legs, walking over to an empty corner of the room. David walked over to me and muttered, "8 to 4, can you believe this? Do you think those other four will ever change their mind?"

116

"Yeah," I said softly back to David. "We're just going to have to comb through all of the evidence and find something that we've missed."

"I don't know. Those four seem pretty set in their ways," David whispered. "Especially Richard and Catherine, they have voted not guilty from the very beginning."

I shook my head and quietly said, "I'm more worried about Nancy. She may be impossible to convince. I don't even know how to go about proving Paul was not framed. I mean, how do you do that?"

"Hey," Max said, coming over to me to shake my hand. As he shook my hand with a very firm grip, Max said, "Good job uncovering that Paul never called for room service. That should have been enough to convince everyone."

"But, it wasn't," David said. "The question is where do we go from here."

"I don't know," I said. "The tough thing is that the four are voting not guilty for different reasons. Richard is voting not guilty because he believes Paul's alibi, Nancy thinks Paul might have been framed, Jonathan just doesn't trust the boys, and Catherine, I don't know, I think she may have a problem putting someone with no prior record to death."

"I say divide and conquer," Max said. "And we should start on Jonathan because he would be easiest to attack. It's obvious those boys are telling the truth. The video supports half the things they say." My eyes widened with Max's remark. "What?" Max asked confused.

David smiled and shook his finger. "You figured something out, didn't you?"

I nodded before walking away to take my seat. Within the next minute, everyone else had taken his or her seats at the table as well. "I'd like to discuss something," I said, turning toward Nancy. "I believe you felt uncomfortable voting guilty because you feared the defendant could have been framed."

Eric J. Lee

Nancy smiled uneasily, possibly caught off guard about being put on the spot. "That's right."

"So, you think someone, whoever, it doesn't matter," I said, waving my hand. "That someone got a red Porsche 914 just like the defendant's, actually keyed it in the exact same spot, then stole the defendant's Chicago Bulls jacket with the hanging thread out of his closet. Then, this person made sure he matched the defendant's height and weight. You think someone went through all this trouble…"

"It's not a lot of trouble if you're trying to commit murder," Nancy said as she leaned forward in her chair.

"Hold on a minute, let me finish my question. Why would someone go through so much trouble to look like the defendant when he was committing this crime?"

"It's pretty obvious," Nancy said, adjusting her glasses. "This someone wanted anyone who saw him that night to think he was actually Paul Sutton."

"I see, so this someone goes through all this trouble to look like Paul Sutton, I mean his disguise is so good he's able to fool two of his students." I raised my eyebrows. "Why then did he destroy the only visible video camera in the liquor store?" The confident look on Nancy's face disappeared. She fell back in her chair, stunned. I continued, "If someone were trying to pose as the defendant to try to frame him, the last thing that someone would do is destroy the video evidence. We all saw the footage from the hidden camera. That was exactly what happened. Thus, I deduce, he wasn't framed."

There was silence in the juror room. All eyes were on Nancy. She took her time as she thought for a while. "Okay, I'm changing my vote to guilty," Nancy announced, which caused Max to clinch his fist in celebration.

"What do you think Richard?" David asked.

"That's a really good point that Robert made," Richard said, stroking his chin. "But, I already believed the prosecution's

118

case. My problem is that the defense has offered an equally believable scenario. I still believe his alibi. And according to our instructions, I must vote not guilty." Howard groaned as David and Max shook their heads in frustration. Any hope of an immediate consensus was dashed.

"How are you feeling, Jonathan?" I asked the youngest member of our jury.

"I don't know," Jonathan said, squinting. "I never really needed to believe that he was framed. I just believed Mrs. Wells testimony that it was a red sports car that came into that parking lot. Look, Brad hated Paul. We all know that. For revenge, he and Alan could have invented that the sports car was a Porsche 914 and that it had a key mark."

"Now, hold it right there," Victoria said. "What about the Bulls jacket with the hanging thread? That's on the video."

"Yes, it is," Jonathan admitted. "But, the Bulls are a popular team. I know a lot of people who have their paraphernalia. It could have been another jacket with the same thread problem. I'm still voting not guilty."

"And you Catherine?" I asked.

"I'm not sure. Robert makes some good points, but I still believe his alibi and the fact remains that he has no past history that shows he's capable of ever planning such an evil act." Catherine nodded as if she was reaffirming her position in her mind. "Yeah, I still have to vote not guilty."

Since Catherine and Richard had stated that they believed the defendant's alibi, Nancy suggested that we switch gears to go over that evidence again. We spent the next half hour going through it in excruciating detail before taking another vote. As expected, it came out 9 to 3 with Richard, Catherine, and Jonathan as the only holdouts.

At that point, everyone agreed to adjourn for lunch. I wanted to be alone with my thoughts so I turned down David's offer for lunch. As I walked out of the building, Catherine asked me what I thought about her knitted sweater. I was impressed and I told her so.

"I still have some work left with this," Catherine said, explaining how the sleeves needed touching up.

"Well, I hope I never see it finished," I said. "I'm hoping we'll be out of here today."

"I hope we just can come to a consensus," Catherine said. "No matter how long it takes and whether we send Paul Herbert Sutton to his classroom or to his death. We've got to get to the right answer."

"Well, we have 12 bright people in there. We will," I said before we parted ways.

I drove to a local restaurant about a mile from the courthouse and had lunch. On the way back, I stopped at a local gas station, got out of the car and began pumping my own gas.

"How are you today, sir?" a voice from behind me said. I turned around and looked at the person who asked me the question. It was a boy around the age of seventeen. I guess he was the attendant. He was well kept and had a nice smile. He reminded me a little of Alan, but I knew it wasn't him. I wondered why he wasn't in school.

"Fine thanks," I said.

"Would you like me to check your oil, sir?" the boy asked.

"No thanks," I said as the gas pump cut off. "Most of the parts of this car are older than you," I joked as I tried to put more gas in my car, wanting to make sure I got my tank completely full.

"You shouldn't top off your car," the boy said. A chill went up my spine. I stared at him. I couldn't believe my ears.

"What did you say?" I asked slowly.

"You shouldn't top off your car sir," the boy repeated. "The pumps are airtight."

"That's it!" I exclaimed, which truly confused the boy. "I need to use your phone. Where's the nearest phone booth?"

The boy gestured toward the nearby building. I paid him for the gas and jogged over to the phone booth to make a call to a friend in the police department. I asked him to look up something for me on his computer. He gave me the information that I needed and I rushed back to the courthouse.

We reassembled in the jury room. Before everyone had even taken a seat, I spoke up. "Over lunch, I uncovered something that proves Paul Sutton is guilty."

"And what's that?" Nancy asked with wrinkled forehead.

I paused as the rest of the standing juror members took their seats. "Who remembers Paul Sutton saying that he saw Alan Clark in the morning on October 15th?"

"I remember that," Laura responded. "Paul was at the gas station."

"Yeah, I have that as well," Nancy said, looking down at her notepad.

"In that encounter, I distinctly remember Paul saying that Alan told him not to top off his gas tank as Paul was filling up."

"What's the point?" Richard said impatiently.

"The point is what was Paul doing right before he was pulled over in Stanislaus that same night?" I asked.

"He was getting gas," David said, beginning to get my point.

"Now, according to Paul's testimony, he left school and went directly home," I said, reviewing the facts. "Then, he headed 100 miles north to Stanislaus. He didn't use his car again until 1:15 when he went out for wine. Now, Bill's liquor store is about 10 miles due South from Stanislaus. The gas station was very close to the liquor store. So, at this point, he has driven a maximum of about 110 miles. On a Porsche 914, you don't need a fill up after 110 miles. But, if Paul drove 100 miles up to Stanislaus, 100 miles back to Kings City, and 90 miles back north to Bill's liquor store, that would be about 290 miles."

Eric J. Lee

"That's about how many miles you could get out of a Porsche 914," Max concurred. "Maybe a little more with highway driving."

"Exactly my point," I said. "I did a little research. Most Porsche 914's get about 25 miles per gallon on the highway, and have 12 gallon tanks. That's 300 miles on a tank of gas. Therefore, the only way Paul would even be thinking of gassing up again is if he drove 290 miles, not 110 miles!"

Richard took a deep breath, apparently reconsidering his position. "I'd like to hear both Paul's and Officer Cummings' testimony again. And if it's exactly as Robert says, I may have to change my verdict."

"I would like that as well," Catherine said while Jonathan appeared to be deep in thought.

It took about an hour. But, we heard both Paul and Officer Cummings' testimony and it was exactly how I remembered. "I suggest we take a vote and let's make it binding," I said, foreseeing that our deliberations were coming to an end.

"Okay, we'll go by show of hands. All those voting guilty," Nancy said. Eleven hands went up. Richard and Jonathan had switched to guilty. "All those voting not guilty?" Nancy asked.

"I'm sorry," Catherine said as she raised her hand. There was a groan among the group. "I have to vote my heart. I still have some big doubts."

"Again with that word, 'doubt'. Is there anything you don't have a doubt about?" Max asked.

Catherine looked away from Max, not dignifying his last comment with a response. "Paul just might have wanted to get gas early."

"It was 1:30 in the morning and the temperature was below freezing. His wife was waiting for him back at the resort on supposedly a romantic night," I argued. "Why would he stop for gas if his tank was two-thirds full?"

122

"Well, what about what Richard said," Catherine retorted. "If Paul went down to Kings City to kill Gary at 11:30 that night, why did it take so long for him to get back to Stanislaus? He got the ticket. It says the time on it."

"It doesn't really matter," Richard said. "We've found inconsistencies and illogical patterns in the defense's alibi."

"Come on," David said. "All eleven of us think that he's guilty. Doesn't that tell you something?"

"Look," Catherine said with a sigh. "I'm not sending someone to his death unless I don't have a reasonable doubt. I don't care what the vote is."

I felt kind of sorry for her because all eleven of us ganged up on her. After another thirty minutes of trying to convince her, we finally all could agree on only one thing- we weren't about to all agree. It was a depressing and frustrating moment. We called the bailiff to tell the judge we were hung.

The judge called us back into the courtroom. Everyone was there: the attorney, the defendant, and the press. The judge asked us if we had reached a unanimous decision. I looked over to Paul. I couldn't help but think he was getting an undeserved reprieve. Nancy rose and said, "Your honor, we, the members of the jury, are unable to reach a unanimous verdict."

The judge frowned and one by one asked each of us if we felt that more deliberations would help us reach a decision. We all said no. The judge got up from his chair and slowly walked over to us. "Ladies and gentlemen, you are serving jury duty. And as the title indicates, it is a duty!" The judge's eyes surveyed all of us as he talked. He spoke authoritatively and with confidence and control. "The fact that you twelve came in here giving up after just twelve hours of deliberations, tells me that you do not take this duty seriously. You all observed the same case, listened to the same testimony, and examined the same exhibits. I don't believe you can give up so quickly and say you can't reach a consensus." The judge looked at his watch. "It's 3:15. I know all of you would like to leave and start your weekend. Well, I've got news for you twelve. I'm NOT declaring this a hung jury. And you can forget about going home soon. I'm not going to even entertain the possibility of a hung jury until after eight p.m. tonight. Do you people think this is some game? A man's life is at stake here. This is jury duty. If I get the slightest notion that one of you is not treating your involvement as a duty, I will hold you in contempt. Dismissed!" I was momentarily shocked. Apparently, my stint as a juror was far from over.

As we all slowly walked back to the juror room, no one said a word. The bailiff let us into the juror room and we all took our seats.

"Can't believe we stuck up here for five more hours," Howard muttered.

"Well, hopefully, it won't be five hours," Richard said. "Maybe if we go over the evidence again we can..."

"We've been over the evidence a thousand times," a tired Max complained. "But, the queen of doubt over there keeps saying she's not convinced."

"There's no reason to be snide," I said to Max.

"You think it is easy to be the only one voting not guilty," Catherine said. "You think I don't want to go home now. It would be easy for me to go along with you eleven people and get home before my favorite television show comes on tonight. What would be hard is living with myself knowing I sent a man who I felt was innocent to his death."

"Catherine, you mentioned sentencing someone to death a few times," I said. "Are you voting not guilty because you have a problem sentencing someone to death?"

"No, that's not it at all," Catherine said, shaking her head. "I can sentence someone to death who is definitely guilty."

I studied Catherine as the room was momentarily quiet. I was unsure whether her answer convinced me.

"Well," Nancy said, breaking the silence. "How do we want to go about this?"

"I think we should focus on the areas that Catherine has the most doubts about and try to address those," David said.

"Wait a minute," Catherine said. "This shouldn't be about changing *my* mind. We should all reexamine the evidence. And vote the way we honestly believe. No matter how anyone else in this room may vote."

"All right," Nancy said with a deep sigh. She looked at Catherine. "What do you suggest we do?"

"I would like to ask a question to Richard and Jonathan."

"Me?" Jonathan asked surprised.

"Yes," Catherine said. "You and Richard voted not guilty earlier. Then, Robert said a few things to the group and now you changed your verdict. Are you two sure about your position?"

"Yes," Richard said. "I'm sure."

Catherine then said, "You're sure of the guilt of this young man who has never been convicted of a crime in his life, and a man who has an alibi, which another person swears is true, because she was with him. You're still sure?"

"Yes," Richard said. "The bottom line is I believe Alan's testimony and we've now found a real error in the defendant's alibi."

"I see," Catherine said before turning to Jonathan. "How about you? Are you sure?"

Jonathan paused for a moment. "Yeah, I am."

"Would you bet your life that you're right?" Catherine asked.

"Excuse me," a startled Jonathan said as he shifted in his seat.

"I asked you if you'd bet your life that Paul is guilty," Catherine repeated.

Jonathan chuckled nervously with the confrontation. "Well, no, I wouldn't bet my life. But that doesn't mean..."

"Wait a minute," Catherine said, holding her hand up. "If you can't bet your own life that you are right, how in good conscience can you bet Paul's?"

Max clapped sarcastically. "Nice speech, but apparently you've forgotten the judge's instructions. He said that the standard to find the defendant guilty is beyond a reasonable doubt. He didn't say anything about betting your life. Now, lady, you're not going to change anyone's mind. So, why don't you just vote guilty like the rest of us so we can get out here?"

"Get out of here?" Catherine repeated in disbelief. "Is that all you can think about?" Max slumped back in his chair and rolled his eyes. Undaunted, Catherine turned and ardently addressed the rest of the group. "Is that what this has become? How quick we can get out of here? We're supposed to be on a search for the truth."

"Calm down," I said to Catherine, who obviously felt isolated and defensive.

"Don't tell me to calm down," Catherine snapped. "Our decision could result in pumping a lethal amount of electricity through a man's body and some people just want to get out of here." Catherine sat back in her chair, folding her arms in front of her chest. The rest of us sat in stunned silence at her outburst.

"I'd like to call for another vote," Jonathan said.

"Okay," Nancy said slowly, still recovering from the shock of Catherine's speech. "We'll go by show of hands again. All those voting guilty." My eyes were on Jonathan as I raised my hand. His hands remained rested on the table. "Not guilty?" Nancy asked. "Catherine and Jonathan raised their hands."

"Unbelievable," Richard said, looking at his watch. "What's going to happen next?"

"This is ridiculous," Max groaned as he looked at the ceiling.

"You want to know why I changed my vote?" Jonathan asked, sitting up in his chair. Victoria nodded her head sternly, causing Jonathan to take a deep breath before saying, "It just seems to me that we have a lot of evidence that it was Paul's car, but not much evidence that Paul was the one in the vehicle."

"Did you sleep through Alan's testimony?" Victoria asked.

"No, I heard it," Jonathan said. "But, I think Alan may have made the same mistake you all are."

"What do you mean by that?" I asked.

"I mean that Alan saw the car too. He knew in his mind that it was his teachers. He may have just assumed that he saw his teacher."

"Assumed!" Max repeated. "What are you talking about? Alan got up there on the stand under oath and swore that he got a good look at the defendant. How can you say that he assumed he saw him? See," Max said, pausing to wag his index finger at all of us. "This is why so many criminals get set free."

The verbal wars continued with the conversation being dominated by Max, Catherine, Victoria, Jonathan and Nancy. I stayed out of it because it had very little had to do with examining the evidence. It felt like we all had made up our mind and there was little chance of anyone changing. I was mentally exhausted. It was approaching six o'clock. It was still two hours before we could approach the judge about the possibility of a hung jury. We decided to forgo taking a long break for dinner. Most of the group agreed that if the judge knew we deliberated for a solid five hours, he would more likely believe that we had given it a serious try and thus would declare it a hung jury.

We did agree to a short break. A few people got up to stretch their legs. I saw Max walk over to a standing Richard and whisper something to him. Then, our eyes met, and Max motioned for me to come over. I reluctantly got up from my

Eric J. Lee

seat and walked over to him. As I approached, Max led me to
the restroom, where Richard was washing his face in the sink.

"What's going on?" I asked as Max locked the bathroom
door behind us.

"Here's the deal," Max said. "We are the three most
persuasive people on this jury. We need to end this, now. I
thought we should game-plan on how we can convince our two
holdouts- the old lady and the kid."

"Their names are Catherine and Jonathan," I said a little
bothered by Max's tone.

"Whatever," Max shot back.

"Look," Richard said, stepping in between us. "I don't
know if this little discussion is appropriate, but, right now, I'm
for anything that gets us out of here." Richard rubbed his chin
for a few seconds. "I say we go after the kid, Jonathan. He's
straddling both sides. I think it would be easier to turn him."

"I like that," Max said nodding. "Catherine's a tough broad.
But, once she's alone for a long period of time, she'll crack."

"Here's what I think we have to do," I said, as if I was a QB
in a football huddle. "We just need to hit Jonathan with the
evidence. He's a college student and he's smart. So, he will
appreciate a logical argument. We just stack the evidence up
one by one until he's overwhelmed."

"We can't let up on him," Richard said. "And we can't let
Catherine or anyone else divert the conversation away from us
laying out a logical argument."

"That includes you too," I said, looking at Max. "Any snide
remarks will just divert attention from our argument and make
them want to dig their heels in even more."

"Okay," Max said, holding both hands in the air. "You got
it." The three of us then headed out of the bathroom and back to
our seats.

"I have something to say," Richard said as everyone took his
or her seat. "Let's get back to the basics. Jonathan, you said,

just a minute ago, that you are voting not guilty because Alan may have only assumed that he saw him."

"That's right. That's what I believe."

"But, there's so much more evidence than Alan identifying the defendant," Richard said. "What about Alan identifying the key mark? And Brad identified it too. And what about Mrs. Wells testifying to seeing a red sports car leave Buckley Liquors?"

"As far as I'm concerned," Catherine said, inserting herself in the conversation. "Since Paul got Brad tossed off the football team, Alan and Brad have reason to implicate him."

Howard shook his head. "Those boys aint lying."

"How do you know that?" Catherine asked.

"How do you know they aren't?" David asked back.

"I don't," Catherine said with exasperation. She paused in attempt to calm down. "I'm not saying that they're lying. I don't know. I'm just saying that they have reason to lie. So, it's reasonable to doubt their testimony."

"I'm sorry to say this," Richard said. "But, I find your logic preposterous."

"Hold on," Max said. "Let's say for a minute because of this football thing that Brad would be mad enough to come to court and commit perjury. But what about Alan?" Max asked with a shoulder shrug. "There was no testimony that said Alan was biased. And it was Alan who not only saw the key mark, but Paul's face. So, how do you explain away Alan's testimony?"

"Here's my answer," Jonathan said speaking up. "Like I said, since he thought he recognized the defendant's car, he could have just assumed it was him. Plus, here's another possibility. I remember what it was like to be in high school. Peer pressure is real. We know how upset Brad was at Paul. He could have exerted influence on his buddy Alan."

There was a deep sigh among the group. I decided to speak. "We are looking at this all wrong. Forget about Alan and Brad for a moment. Forget Mrs. Wells. Forget Dr. Baculi's report. Even forget the Bulls jacket with the hanging thread. At nine o'clock, the defendant admits to being with his car in Stanislaus." I walked over to pick up People's Exhibit #7, Paul Sutton's traffic ticket. "At 1:55 a.m., we know that Paul Sutton and his car were ten miles south of Stanislaus. The question is where was his car between 9:00 PM and 1:55 AM. We have two eye-witnesses saying they're sure they saw it and the key mark at the crime scene. And a third could describe a similar car. Do you guys really believe that you have a reasonable basis to think that all three people are wrong about the car?" Jonathan scratched his head as Catherine looked down at the table. "And there's one more thing," I said slowly. "We know that the defendant's car did not just stay in Stanislaus as Paul claimed. For Paul to be gassing the car up at 1:55 AM, his tank had to be on empty. Since he gassed up that morning and testified that he left school to go directly to Stanislaus, we know his car did a lot more traveling. And a trip back down to Kings City and then back up toward Stanislaus would do it."

The room was silent for a moment as it appeared Catherine and Jonathan were reconsidering their positions. "Maybe someone besides Paul drove his car down to Kings City," Catherine said.

"Who?" Richard asked. "The person would have to have taken his car and gotten it back before Paul left to get wine. And Paul testified to having an alarm on his car."

"What if it was his wife?" Jonathan said softly. "She would have known how to disarm the alarm."

"Nope, that's not possible," Richard said. "Remember, Doctor Baculi's report. Gloria isn't male and she doesn't fit either weight or height classification."

"You guys are looking too hard," Max said. "The truth is right there in front of you. Paul is the one who drove his car. Paul is the one who fits the description in Dr. Baculi's report.

Paul is the one who Alan saw there. It was Paul's Chicago Bulls jacket that matches the one on videotape. And Paul is the one who got a ticket while he was rushing back!"

There was a noticeable pause. There was obvious tension in the room, but there was hope we had made a breakthrough. It was seven o'clock. We decided to take another vote.

"All those voting guilty," Nancy asked. Ten hands immediately shot up and another one slowly followed. The slow hand was Jonathan's. He had changed his mind again, switching back to guilty.

"All those voting not guilty?" Nancy asked, although the answer was already clear.

Catherine slowly raised her hand, glaring at Jonathan as if he had betrayed her. Richard got up from the table to either stretch or relieve some frustration. Thinking this was an impromptu break, I got up and stretched both arms in the air. I knew one thing. We had exactly an hour to try to convince Catherine. Otherwise, we'd be back to court to say that we were still hung. I walked over to the small window. My whole body was tired: my legs, my back, even my eyes.

"This next hour is going to be a waste of time," David whispered to me as he joined me by the window. "She won't budge."

"You never know," I whispered. "We turned Richard and Nancy, and we've convinced Jonathan twice."

"I admit that you have worked some magic so far," David said softly. "But, I can tell. Catherine's mind is made up."

"Alright!" Victoria exclaimed, getting everyone's attention. Everyone in the juror room stopped their conversations and looked at Victoria. "If everyone could please sit down," Victoria said, holding her right hand on her forehead. Once we all took our seats, Victoria looked at Catherine said, "We have exactly an hour. Tell us what you need discussed to possibly get to a guilty verdict."

Eric J. Lee

Catherine paused a moment to gather her thoughts. "You're asking me to put a man behind bars, possibly to his death. And who is this man? He's never been suspected of a crime before. And he's a school teacher. Not a drug dealer. Or a gang member. He's a school teacher."

"You're showing pity," Nancy said, obviously exhausted. "The judge said we're not supposed to rule based on pity."

"And his profession is completely irrelevant," Richard said. "You're not supposed to consider it. The judge would tell you that if you asked him."

"Well, apparently you guys are all experts on what the judge thinks," Catherine said. "But it doesn't matter what the judge thinks, it matters what I think."

The next hour was a disaster. We made absolutely no progress. Most of the time was spent attacking Catherine. Several times, Laura and I had to stick up for her integrity.

At eight o'clock, we decided to go back into the courtroom and the judge again asked if we felt more deliberations would be useful. We all agreed that it wouldn't. The judge nodded and grudgingly declared that he had a hung jury. I watched Paul closely. He smiled, perhaps knowing he wasn't going to jail at least for another couple of months. He and his wife embraced. The judge thanked us for our service and let us know that our jury duty had ended. The attorneys grabbed us as we walked out of the courtroom, interested in what our thoughts were and the vote counts on the verdicts. Most of us stayed to tell them. I said a personal good-bye to David and Laura. I also told Catherine that I admired her for sticking to what she believed, even though I disagreed with her. It was strange. I would probably never see any of them again.

Just about everyone had left when I approached the prosecuting attorney. He introduced himself as Clarence and said, "You're the private eye."

"That's right," I said. "I need to know. Are you going to try the case again?"

"Well, that's going to be up to the D.A.," Clarence responded with a shrug. "I heard your vote was 11-1. I wonder how Barbara, the woman who we had to replace, would've voted."

"Guilty. No doubt about it. She said she didn't trust Paul because his face reminded her of her ex-husband."

"She discussed the case before deliberations?" Clarence asked in shock, suffering from a heavy dose of idealism. My nod answered his question. "Well, I'm surprised someone from Sierra Heights didn't have more sympathy for Paul."

"Barbara lived in Sierra Heights?" I said with raised eyebrows, knowing it to be an upscale neighborhood.

"Yep. Probably got a nice divorce settlement from that ex-husband you were talking about. You know, nice house, new car, the whole bit."

"Well, the car couldn't have been too new because she dropped out due to engine problems." Clarence nodded his head in agreement. At that moment, a thought jumped into my mind. "Oh my God! Barbara does have a new car, a brand new car."

"That doesn't make sense," Clarence said as his forehead wrinkled. My jaw dropped as a realization hit me. "What's the matter?"

"Maybe nothing," I said, not wanting to mention anything until I was more sure. My theory though could be verified if he told me what was found on the victim when the police arrived. Clarence said he wasn't sure.

"Tell you what," he said. "I'm working tomorrow. Sometimes, talking to jurors can provide a fresh perspective on the evidence." He handed me his business card. "Call me around ten to set up a time to come in, if you're interested."

"Okay," I said slowly. "I'll come down, if you look up what was found on Gary Bender's body."

Clarence looked puzzled, but he shrugged his shoulders. "Fine, I'll have that information when we talk tomorrow."

I called Clarence around ten on Saturday morning. It was funny. I thought my interest and involvement in Paul Sutton's case would end with my jury stint. But, I had a feeling the most interesting part had yet to come.

"Did you check the police report to determine what was found on Gary Bender?" I asked immediately.

"Oh yeah," Clarence said as I could hear some pages being shuffled. "Not much to speak of on Gary according to the police report. They found a wallet with twenty-two bucks in it, some major credit cards, and miscellaneous ID like driver's license."

"That's it, nothing else?"

"Yep, that's it. What else did you expect?"

"What about keys," I said. "Especially, house keys."

"Not on him, according to the police report," Clarence responded.

I now realized I was right. I explained to Clarence and he was astonished that he didn't see it before. I told him it may be even more complicated than that, but I would have to ask Barbara Hendricks a few questions to confirm my suspicion.

"Barbara?" Clarence asked. "What does she have to do with anything?"

"I'll let you know when I see you. Let's say at noon."

"Noon is fine, but what's this about Barbara?"

"I'll tell you later," I repeated, before hanging up the phone. I looked up Barbara's address in the phone book and decided to pay her a visit. I rang the doorbell and Barbara answered the door, seemingly shocked to see me.

"I know you," she said, pointing at me. "You were on that jury. I read the newspaper. I can't believe you guys couldn't convict him."

"I'd like to know why you couldn't make it to jury duty and thus got dropped."

"Car wouldn't start up. Had to call a tow truck and get it sent to a mechanic." She paused before asking, "And why do you care?"

"Well, I think Paul got help from an accomplice," I said. "But, I need to know some information about your car to be sure. It is a new car. Right?"

"An accomplice, eh," Barbara said, folding her arms. "I think you've been watching too many Sherlock Holmes movies. But, if you must know, yeah. It was a new car. Bought it new a month ago."

"What was wrong with the car?"

Barbara chuckled. "Now, I don't know nothin' about cars. But, my mechanic says the spark plug wire, or something like that, was cut. Probably some high school kids playing a prank."

"Or someone else," I said under my breath. Barbara looked puzzled as I thanked her and left.

After running a background check on Paul's accomplice on my office computer, I rushed to the prosecuting attorney's office for my appointment with Clarence.

Once I arrived at his office, he escorted me into a conference room. I was surprised to see a portly officer wearing a brown hat awaiting us. It was the arresting officer Sgt. James Griffin. Clarence introduced us and we all took our seats.

"Well, thanks for coming down here," Clarence said. "Sgt. Griffin and I were just interested in hearing some of your thoughts on the case. You think he's guilty, right?"

"I know he's guilty," I said sternly.

"Now how do you *know* that he's guilty?" Sgt. Griffin asked with a smirk on his face. I explained the fact that for Paul to be gasing up that night, his car had to travel back to Kings City.

"Wow," Sgt. Griffin said in deep thought. "Maybe this will convince the D.A. to try the case again."

"No," Clarence said, shaking his head. "There's no changing his mind."

"The D.A. doesn't want to try this case again?" I asked. "Why?"

Sgt. Griffin and Clarence looked at each other as if they were deciding what to say. However, I think they realized that they already had given it away. Clarence let out a noticeable sigh and said, "The D.A. took a lot of heat for going after the senator's husband. We guaranteed a conviction and we didn't get it. It was made very clear to us. We were only going to get one shot."

"So, you're just going to let him walk when the jury unanimously voted guilty except for Catherine," I said. "And there's something I have to tell you about her." I explained to Sgt. Griffin and Clarence the information that I had gathered. Although the two were impressed, Clarence adamantly felt that it was not going to change the D.A.'s decision not to retry the case.

Clarence had an idea: to call Paul Sutton down to the station Monday morning and try to entice him into a plea bargain. He asked me whether I would be willing to come in to help.

"Sure, but there's one more thing. You know how you said in court that Paul had so little money and the victim had so much more than he should." Clarence nodded his head before I said dramatically, "I think Paul was being blackmailed by the victim." Clarence and Sgt. Griffin looked at each other. Before they could speak, I continued, "The most likely thing that the victim would be able to blackmail for is an affair. On Monday morning, you need to tell Paul that you know about the affair and will bring it up when you re-try the case."

"No, no way," Clarence said.

"What? Why not?"

"You think we didn't consider that Paul was being blackmailed," Clarence said. "We didn't bring it up because we couldn't find any hard evidence of either an affair or blackmail. No checks were written to Gary Bender." Clarence wagged his index finger in the air as he said to me, "Listen, the Suttons are very powerful people. One mention of an affair and they will sue for defamation of character."

"Defamation of character?" I said confused. "You aren't going to go public with it. You'll just threaten to."

"They'll see it as an empty threat," Clarence said. "Besides, there are other things I have to worry about."

"Like what?" Sgt. Griffin asked.

"My career, for one. If I make the slightest mis-step, their attorney could have me dis-barred."

I shook my head in disappointment. "At least let me…"

"No, end of discussion," Clarence snapped. "No one is going to mention anything about blackmail or an affair." With that, Clarence left the room.

On Monday morning, I was back at the police station. Clarence explained my role, with instructions to observe through a window in the adjacent room until I was called.

He looked me straight in the eye and said, "When you come into the room, I only want you to talk about what Catherine said during deliberations. That's it, okay?"

"Yes," I replied.

Clarence tilted his head slightly before adding, "Not a word about blackmail or an affair. Got it?"

I nodded and Clarence left to head into the interrogation room. Paul was already waiting there with his attorney. They were sitting at the table when Clarence entered the room.

Still standing, Clarence spoke first. "The jury's vote was 11-1 and you know what that means."

"That there was only one intelligent person on the jury," Paul quipped.

Eric J. Lee

"No. It means that we're going to try your case again."

"You're bluffing," the defense attorney said. "There's no way you'd try this case again. The court of public opinion is against you. The D.A. is getting lambasted in the papers."

"You've got it wrong," Clarence said. "We will try this case again, and this time we'll get a conviction."

"Why did you call us down here?" Paul's attorney asked.

Clarence took a seat opposite Paul and said to him, "We're prepared to offer you a deal. Twenty years. You'll be a free man with about thirty more years to live once you get out. Plus, complete immunity for your wife as an accomplice."

"No, no deal," the defense attorney said. "You're only making this deal because you're desperate. I don't think the D.A. is letting you try this case again."

"What do you think, Paul?" Clarence asked. "This deal expires when you walk out of this room."

"I think you're crazy. I won't agree to one day in jail."

"We'll see about that," Clarence said. He turned and said into the speakerphone, "Bring them in." Paul looked at his attorney, who was glaring at Clarence.

I was escorted in the room by Sgt. Grifin. About twenty seconds passed before Catherine Fenton, escorted by another policeman, entered the room. Not noticing Paul or me, she immediately said to Sgt. Griffin, "You call me down here and then have me waiting for a half an hour. What's going on?"

Sgt. Griffin didn't answer and Catherine looked around. She appeared taken aback to see me. But more importantly, she seemed in shock to see Paul. Catherine carried with her, her knitting bag. It was amazing. The sweater she had been knitting was almost complete. Everything pieced perfectly into place, I guess, much like this mystery.

"Why don't you have a seat ma'am," Sgt. Griffin said to Catherine. She slowly sat down. "Mrs. Fenton, did you know Paul Sutton before the trial?"

"No."

"Of course not," Sgt. Griffin said. "Cause you took an oath, with the penalty of perjury, that you didn't know the defendant or any of the witnesses. You remember that, right?"

"Yes," Catherine responded.

"Unfortunately," Sgt. Griffin said. "The prosecuting attorney doesn't believe you, and he's prepared to prosecute you for perjury unless you tell us the truth."

"I don't think you should question Mrs. Fenton until she has counsel," Paul's attorney asserted.

"I don't need counsel," Catherine said. "I haven't done anything wrong."

Clarence looked over to me and I walked up to Catherine. "Catherine, I think you knew Paul before the trial. You used his full name, Paul Herbert Sutton, the first day of deliberations."

Catherine smiled, but under that smile I could sense nervousness. "If I said that," Catherine said slowly. "I probably read it in the newspaper. All because you know a famous person's middle name, it doesn't prove you know them."

"It would if you couple that with the fact that you were next door neighbors for nine years," I said. I had researched that fact on my office computer. "It was in the city of Pinewoods about 30 years ago. It's just a hunch. But, perhaps when young Paul would get in trouble, his mother would do what a lot of mothers do. She'd shout out his full name, Paul Herbert Sutton." Catherine remained silent, just shaking her head. "During one of the breaks early in the trial, you defended Paul saying he wasn't born with a silver spoon in his mouth. I wondered how you would know that. Now, I know. Pinewood wasn't a wealthy city."

Catherine glanced over at Paul who simply stared straight ahead. "Listen, that was over 30 years ago. If he did live next to me as you say, he would have been a just a kid. I didn't talk to the kids in Pinewood. I thought they were a nuisance."

Clarence stepped forward and motioned me to step back. "I will ask you one last time. Did you know Paul before the trial?"

Catherine stared at Clarence for a few seconds before saying forcefully, "No."

"In light of what Mr. Douglas has said, we will be charging you with perjury. That will run up to a year in jail, if you're convicted. You should rethink securing counsel. Book her," Clarence said before Sgt. Griffin led a tight-lipped Catherine out of the room.

"We really enjoyed that little performance," the defense attorney said. "Whatever you were trying didn't work. Do you have any more questions for my client?"

Clarence looked at me and then back to Paul. "No, you're free to go. But, think long and hard before you leave. When we re-try, we're going to add jury tampering to the list of charges. You'll definitely be looking at the death penalty. Once you leave, that plea bargain of 20 years is off the table, as is immunity for your wife as a conspirator and Catherine for perjury."

"I'm not interested in a plea bargain," Paul said rising. "I'm innocent and I'm leaving." Clarence dropped his head as Paul headed for the door.

I spoke on emotion as I shouted, "We know about the affair." Paul stopped in his tracks and Clarence glared at me.

Paul slowly turned around. "What are you talking about?"

"Gary Bender was blackmailing you and your wife. That's why you two had so little money and Gary had so much. Your wife had an affair with Gary."

"You have proof of an affair?" the defense attorney asked. "Do you have proof of blackmail? Because if you don't, we'll slap you with a lawsuit for libel before you can say, 'I'm sorry'."

Clarence was about to intervene, but I spoke before he could. "You know it's ironic," I said, looking at Paul. "You worked so hard to keep your wife's affair a secret. I mean, you paid thousands of dollars to hide it. You even murdered a man so word of the affair didn't get out. Now, the only way to keep the secret, is to confess and take this plea bargain."

"We can make that part of the plea," Clarence said. "Neither the blackmail nor the affair will be in any records or dispensed to the public."

I said, "It comes down to what kind of man you are. Are you a man who killed to save his woman from being taken advantage of by some con artist? Are you a man who committed murder for his own selfish reasons and don't care if his wife's name gets dragged the mud? And don't care that it sends another woman to jail for perjury?"

"You don't know what you're talking about," Paul said.

"But I do," I said. "You can leave now and take the major risk that you won't get convicted. But, this time you won't get a confidant on the jury. This time, your wife is going to be humiliated and her career will be over. This time, you'll wind up on death row."

"Okay, that's enough," the defense attorney said. "This conversation is over." She turned toward Paul. "Let's go."

"Hold on," Paul said to his attorney before turning toward me with angry eyes. "You don't know me. I'm a good man."

"Well, actions speak louder than words," I said. "Do the right thing. If you leave this room, the opportunity to ease the pain of others goes away forever."

"Alright, that's it, we're going," the defense attorney said. The defense tugged at Paul's arm, but he didn't budge as both of his eyes were fixated on me. Seeing she was unable to move him, she turned toward Clarence. "Discussions with my client will end now. I am leaving and I forbid any communications to occur with my client without me present. Is that clear?"

"Yes," Clarence said. He looked at me. "Say nothing more."

The defense attorney started for the door when Paul said, "You're fired."

The defense attorney stopped abruptly and slowly turned around. "Excuse me?"

"I want to talk to them," Paul said. "And if you're no longer my attorney, you can't stop me."

"Paul, you're making a terrible mistake."

"If you still want to be my attorney, then sit down and say nothing unless I ask you." She sat back down and Paul said to Clarence, "You sign a written agreement not to prosecute my wife and Catherine, and you promise in writing that the details of the plea will not be leaked, then I'll agree to twenty years."

"Sure, but you'll have to tell us everything."

"I will, as soon as it's all in writing and my lawyer has reviewed it. And one more thing, I'd like him to leave," Paul said, pointing at me.

Clarence looked at me and gestured with his head. I slowly got up and left the room.

A week passed without a word from Sgt. Griffin or Clarence Mann. The local papers reported that Paul agreed to a plea bargain. There was no mention of blackmail or an affair, or any wrongdoing by Catherine or his wife. It was late one evening when my doorbell rang. I was shocked to see Clarence standing at my front door.

"May I come in?" he asked.

"Sure," I said, motioning him to come inside. We sat down in my living room. "Can I get you something to drink?"

"That won't be necessary," he said. "Look, I really shouldn't be here. And I have to admit that I wanted to knock you out when you brought up the affair and blackmail in front of Paul."

"Yeah, sorry about that."

"Don't be. Without it, we never would have gotten his confession. Because you were such a big help, I felt you deserved to hear it firsthand." Clarence, holding a small tape recorder, pushed play. I immediately recognized Paul's voice. "It all started about three years ago. Gary was a snake, a low life. I believe over the course of three, four months he made his best attempt to meet and get to know my wife. And in a weak moment, he seduced her." There was a considerable pause; apparently Paul was having some difficulty continuing. "They had sex and that sleazeball Gary videotaped the whole thing!" I flashed back to how Gary adeptly set up the hidden camera at Buckley Liquors. Paul continued, "He made several copies of the tape and said that he would distribute it to every media outlet in the country unless we paid him blackmail. It wasn't much money at first, but he kept demanding more. He knew the tapes would ruin Gloria's political career. People were even talking about her as a candidate for President. So when her Senate re-election came around, Gary demanded even more. He wanted $10,000 a month. We couldn't afford that. We tried to reason with him, but he said if he didn't get the first $10,000 by Halloween, he'd take his tapes to the media."

"Gary left us no choice. My wife's political career is something she's worked hard for her entire life. I couldn't just stand by and let that sleaze destroy it. So, I did something about it. After Gary's phone call on October 8th demanding more money, I made reservations at the resort. I knew that would be my alibi." As I listened to Paul explain what happened, he seemed to show little remorse and even seemed to be relieved to tell the story he'd been hiding for so long. He continued, "I left the resort out the back way to make sure Pete Kelly didn't see me. I didn't see Alan and Brad at Buckley Liquors. Man! I thought I looked around before I put my mask on."

There was a relatively long pause on the tape. Paul must have been collecting his thoughts before he said, "I knew he kept those tapes at his house. So, after I shot him, I got his house keys out of his pants' pockets. When I got to Gary's house, I searched the entire house. It took awhile, but I found those evil tapes and I destroyed them." I realized that Paul just answered Richard's question of why the prosecution's timeline was off by fifty minutes. "I headed back to Stanislaus. I thought I had enough gas to make it back, but once I got into town, I was on E. The last thing I wanted to do was run out of gas." Paul laughed, seemingly a laugh from an exhausted, frustrated man. "If I just didn't stop, I wouldn't have gotten that ticket. And I wouldn't have had to make up that dumb story about getting wine."

"So, what role did Catherine play?" asked another voice.

"Well, my wife, being a senator and all, was able to pull a few strings and get Catherine and a couple of other people into jury duty at the exact time that my case was up. It was luck though that she got called to my case. I made sure that we threw jurors out until Catherine was picked. Once she was a juror, she warned me about Barbara. I never would get an acquittal with her on the jury. So, late one night, I cut the spark plug wire on her car."

"Well, that's it," Clarence said, turning the tape recorder off.

"Thanks for coming by," I said as we walked to the door.

Once we reached the front door, he turned and said, "It was the least I could do. You were a big help. You know, if there is ever anything that I could do to help you, let me know."

I smiled. "There is one thing."

"And what's that?" Clarence said with a laugh, not expecting me to come up with a favor so quickly.

"It's simple. Get me exempted from jury duty for the rest of my life."

The Return of Henry Burrows

Ex-Inspector Henry Burrows' heartbeat quickened and a series of memories flashed through his mind as he walked through the police station. The clapping of his shoes on the familiar hardwood floors was music to Henry's ears and comforted his soul. Thirty years as chief inspector had a way of affecting a man profoundly. His face lit up when a few veteran officers stopped to greet him with pats on the back and firm handshakes. It had been a long time since he had even set foot in the station, but it was as if he never left.

Henry had a lunch appointment with an old friend, Lt. James Harper. James, a tall intimidating figure, had a squarish face and a smattering of gray hairs sprinkled among his full head of black hair.

Henry stopped in the doorway of James' office, clearing his throat to announce his arrival.

James looked up and instinctively smiled. "Henry! Wow, it's noon already. I'm so sorry. I've got to witness the interrogation of two suspects. Their lawyers just arrived."

"Oh. Do you want to reschedule?"

"I'm sorry," James said with a pained expression.

Just then, a young female officer tapped on the window of the open door and poked her head in. The twenty something officer had short, red hair. She was in full police uniform, with

matching blue pants and shirt. "Sorry to interrupt. They're
waiting for you in room 2."

"Be there in a minute." She nodded and started to leave
until James said, "Wait for a second." He turned toward Henry.
"This may sound crazy, but how would you like to observe the
interrogation? Shouldn't take long, and I'd love to get your gut
reaction."

"You might not have heard," Henry said with a smirk. "I'm
retired."

"But you miss the satisfaction of solving a case," James said,
wagging his index finger. "I'll give you a taste of that without
all the boring paperwork. The case is straightforward. I could
brief you in a couple of minutes. I really could use that
legendary Henry Burrows' intuition."

Henry rubbed his chin as he contemplated James' offer.
Some men might have been afraid to risk tarnishing a legendary
reputation. But, nothing scared old Henry Burrows, not stress,
not murder, and not the risk of failure. The adrenaline began to
flow through his body as he slowly nodded. "Sure, I'll do it."

"Great," James said with a smile. James introduced Henry
to the female officer whose name was Officer Stewart. "Okay,"
James said with a clap of his hands. "First, our characters. We
have three thieves. The masterminds…," James said, flashing
air quotes before continuing, "…are Paul Cooper and Darren
Foster, both in their late forties. Paul used to work at a jewelry
store before he got fired. He has a prior record of theft, but
never any violence. My guess is Paul approached Darren, whom
he currently worked with in a department store, about robbing
his former employer. They needed a third so they brought in
Darren's 19 year old son, Bobby Foster. Here's what happened.
Wearing black clothing and ski masks, they broke in the store
early this morning, before it opened. But, in the process, they
trip a silent alarm. When the first squad car on the scene arrives,
the thieves make a run for it. One takes off in one direction and

two in another. The first officer on the scene, who was Officer Stewart here, ran after two of the thieves down a long alley, yelling for them to stop. One does, but the other keeps running, right?"

"That's right," Officer Stewart said. "The one that stopped turned around. I yelled for him to get his hands up in the air. The next thing I know the fleeing suspect stopped and fired a shot. It hit the other suspect in the back and he collapsed on the ground."

"Whoa," Henry said.

"Turns out the bullet entered the victim's back and exited out his chest," James said.

"Unfortunately, the gunman took off," Officer Stewart said. "I stayed with the injured suspect until backup arrived. With the gunman at least fifty feet away and wearing a mask just before dawn, I can't identify which of the two men we have in custody was the gunman."

"Well, did the suspect who was shot survive?" Henry asked.

"He lost consciousness after he was shot, but he was alive," Officer Stewart replied.

James said, "He's in critical condition, but we have an officer waiting at the hospital in case he regains consciousness."

"Can I see a picture of the gunshot victim?" Henry asked.

"Sure," James said, handing Henry a file.

Henry opened the file and saw a series of pictures of the crime scene. Several pictures showed a body lying face down with a gunshot wound in the back, but one showed a once vibrant, physically fit kid.

"Real pity," Officer Stewart said, looking over Henry's shoulder. "We have to find out which one of these two men did this."

Adrenaline again pumped through Henry's body. The passion and drive were back as if he were still on the force.

"Are we 100% sure that the men we have in custody are the thieves?" Henry asked.

"Yes," James said. "When more officers arrived, we caught both suspects with some of the stolen jewelry within the next half hour. They had ditched the masks, but their clothing was a match on the jewelry store's security camera."

"A security camera?" Henry said. "Doesn't the tape show which exit each man took out of the store?"

"No" James said. "There was only one camera and it shot only the front counter."

"The camera did get good shots of each of the suspects with their masks on at one time or another," Officer Stewart said. "Plus, they still had some of the stolen jewelry on them. It's an open and shut case on the burglary charge."

James paused before adding, "But only one of them even knows that the kid got shot."

"And that's the gunman," Henry said, exhaling audibly.

A row of cushioned chairs in the observation room had a perfect view into the interrogation room, with the help of a two-way mirror. A black-shirted man sat next to another man in a blue suit; the latter likely the man's lawyer. Two detectives, dressed in slacks and a tie, were also in the room. One sat down at the table, the other stood near the door.

James whispered to Henry, "The man on the left is our suspect. He's Darren Foster, the father of the kid who was shot." Calm and composed, Darren's clasped hands rested on the table. Darren was clean-shaven and had short black hair.

In the interrogation room, the lawyer was the first to speak. "Before we get started, I want it noted that my client has no prior convictions. So, off the record, if you're willing to show some leniency and avoid a messy trial, my client might be willing to confess."

"Forget it counselor," the detective responded. "I'm not in a lenient mood when an attempted murder is involved."

"Murder?" the lawyer said. "What are you talking about?"

"We have an eyewitness who saw someone matching your client's description in the exact location your client was in, shoot Bobby Foster."

"What?" Darren said, sitting up in his chair. All of the composure that he showed before, quickly disappeared. Darren put his hand over his heart. "My son, Bobby, was shot? Is he all right?"

"No, he's not. He's in critical condition at the hospital."

Darren buried his face in his hands for a moment. He looked up and asked, "Who shot him?"

"Well, Bobby was fleeing the scene along with another man wearing black pants, black shirt and a mask," the detective said. "When the police instructed Bobby to stop, he complied. But the other man kept running. Once the gunman realized that Bobby was surrendering, he stopped and shot Bobby." Darren gritted his teeth and seemed to turn a dark shade of red. "That means that either you or your partner, Paul Cooper, shot him.

Darren glared with hatred in his eyes, but didn't speak. Darren's lawyer whispered something in his ear, but Darren cut him off saying, "No, I'm talking." Darren turned to the detective. "You can't possibly think that I would shoot my own son. No, it had to be Paul. That lowlife. You cops better nail him for this."

"Why would Paul shoot your son?" the detective asked.

"Why? How should I know? Maybe he was worried a surrendering Bobby would rat him out. That guy would do anything to save his own hide." Darren paused for a moment and his eyes began to well up. "My gosh, it's my fault. If I didn't get Bobby involved in all this, he never would have been there." Darren put his head down on the table as his lawyers rubbed his shoulder. This seemed to remind Darren that he was in an interrogation room. He sat back up and slowly composed himself before saying, "I hope you know Paul's a marksman. I saw him once at a shooting range. He owns several handguns."

"And for the record, how's your expertise with guns?"

"I didn't shoot my son!" Darren exclaimed. Noticing that he had raised his voice, Darren paused to regain his composure. "To answer your question, I have no expertise whatsoever with guns. I've only shot a gun once in my life, the time I was with Paul. I couldn't hit the broad side of a barn."

"Hmm," the detective said, jotting down some notes. "So, when the police arrived and you took off, you weren't with either Bobby or Paul?"

"No," Darren replied. "I ran out the back exit. Bobby and Paul, they must have gone out one of the side exits. Before I say any more, I want to talk to my son. I need to know he's alright."

"Let's move to Paul Cooper's interrogation," James said from the observation room.

"Okay, I'm ready for bachelor #2," Henry said as he and James settled into the adjacent observation room. In the interrogation room, Paul Cooper sat next to what appeared to be his female attorney. Carrying a persona of a tough guy with the girth to match, Paul was over six feet tall and at least 50 pounds overweight. He sported a shaved head, mustache, and goatee. He sat with an arrogant slouch and a menacing sneer, having no respect for the formality or the seriousness of the situation.

The detective walked into the room, "Well, Paul Cooper, you seemed to have gotten yourself in a whole heap of trouble."

"So, I lifted a few pieces of jewelry from that store," Paul said with a shrug.

"Well, since you are in the confessing mood, perhaps you'd like to admit to shooting Bobby Foster?"

Paul paused to scowl at the detective. "What are you cops trying to pull?" Paul shifted in his chair and folded his arms in front of his chest. "Nobody shot Bobby."

"Yeah, they did," the detective said with a sigh. "He's in critical condition at the hospital right now."

"Well, I sure didn't shoot 'im. When the police came, I took off out of one of the side exits. Never saw Bobby after that."

"Well, the fact is that we have an eyewitness who saw Bobby fleeing the scene along with another man wearing black pants, black shirt and a mask. Now that sounds a lot like you."

"Maybe your eyewitness needs glasses," Paul said. "I didn't leave with Bobby."

"Uh huh," the detective said with a look of disbelief. "When the police instructed Bobby to stop, he complied. But whoever was with Bobby kept running. Then, later once he realized that Bobby was surrendering, he stopped and shot him. We think the person fleeing with Bobby was you."

"And this fantasy world that you live in, what would Paul's motive be?" Paul's attorney asked.

"I'll tell you what his motive was," the detective said. He looked directly at Paul. "You knew Bobby was surrendering. You were worried he would implicate you." There was silence in the room as Paul just stared back at the detective. "What's the matter, Paul? You've got nothing to say?"

"Here's what I got to say," Paul said. "Looks like good ol' Darren offed his son."

"But that doesn't make too much sense," the detective said. "Why would Darren shoot his own son? I mean, he loved his son, right?"

"Well, those two were thick as thieves," Paul chuckled evilly.

"You think this is funny, Mr. Cooper. I wonder if you'll have the same sense of humor when we charge you with attempted murder."

"Hey!" Paul shouted, sitting up in his chair and pounding the desk. "I didn't shoot nobody!" The detective took a step closer to see if Paul was about to become violent. Paul slumped back in his chair, holding his hands in the air defensively. The detective took a step back and Paul said calmly, "Darren's your guy."

"The eyewitness only heard one gunshot. And it found its target in Bobby's back," the detective said before pausing to glare at Paul. "Sounds like the work of a marksman. And word is that you're the gun expert and Darren's a novice."

Paul chuckled again. "Hey, look I'm not a cop. Didn't you guys go to school and learn how to put facts together? Here, let me help you out." Paul sat up in his chair again and leaned forward, resting his elbows on the table. "Darren loves his kid. He doesn't want to have his son get caught. When he sees that he will, he aims at the cop." Paul pointed his right index finger and stuck his right thumb in the air. "Bang! But, since he's a lousy shot, he misses and hits his kid."

James looked at Henry with raised eyebrows before motioning to return to his office.

James closed his office door and looked at Henry. "Well, what do you think?"

"I had a question for Officer Stewart," Henry said. "Can you call her in?" James nodded and a minute later she entered the room. "When you were pursuing the suspects, and before the kid stopped, who was in the lead?"

"Pardon?" Officer Stewart said, slightly cocking her head.

"Well, was Bobby running behind the gunman, was the gunman leading Bobby, or were the two running side by side?"

Officer Stewart paused to think for a moment before saying, "The gunman was leading Bobby, but Bobby wasn't too far behind."

"Hmm," Henry said, deep in thought. Seeing a lull in the conversation, James said to Officer Stewart, "Well, thanks for your help. That will be all for now."

She nodded and left, closing the door behind her. James walked back behind his desk and sat down. Henry, who was still deep in thought, stared at the floor as he scratched the back of his head. "Well," James said. "What does that world famous intuition tell you? Darren Foster or Paul Cooper?"

Henry looked back at James. "I'd like to see a diagram of the jewelry store. Has that been done yet?"

"Yes, I have it right here," James said, as he shuffled through papers at his desk. "Here it is," James said, handing it to Henry.

"Hmm," Henry said, looking at the diagram. "Officer Stewart came through the front entrance, right?"

"That's right. She had to break through the door."

Henry continued to study the diagram, which showed a back exit and two side exits on opposite walls. "Let's suppose Darren Foster went out the back exit and Paul Cooper ran out one of the side exits. The question is which of the exits would Bobby Foster take?"

Just then, James' phone rang. "One second," James said, pointing at Henry before picking up the phone.

"James speaking. Hi Kevin, hold on a minute, let me put you on speaker." James pressed the phone against his chest and said to Henry, "This is the officer that we had at the hospital." He hit the speaker button and hung up the phone. "Go ahead Kevin."

"Well, the bad news is that the doctors just informed me that Bobby has died," Kevin said, which caused James cover his face in frustration. "However, about twenty minutes ago, he did regain consciousness for about 30 seconds and I asked him who shot him."

"What did he say?" James asked immediately.

"He was speaking very softly," Kevin said. "But, the best I can make out, he just said the word: 'please'."

"Please?" James said, confused. "Please what?"

"That's it," Kevin responded.

James' forehead wrinkled before he asked, "He just said the word please, spelled P-L-E-A-S-E?"

"Yeah, the best I could tell," Kevin said. "I asked him again, but he didn't respond. He either didn't have the strength to finish his sentence or didn't really understand what I was asking him."

"Okay. Anything else?"

"No," Kevin said, before James hung up.

"Did that make any sense to you?" James asked Henry.

"Actually, it does," Henry said to a shocked James. A smile curled on Henry's lips. "I know who shot Bobby."

James' jaw dropped. "You do? Who?"

"Mind if I tell you how I know first."

"Sure," James said, now an eager listener.

"The only one I trust among these three men is Bobby," Henry said. "I mean, I know he wasn't the gunman. He didn't shoot himself in the back and make the gun disappear. So, we know we can rely on what Bobby said and did as concrete facts."

"What are you talking about? Bobby was the only one of the three you never heard from."

"I don't need to hear from him to know what he did," Henry said. "Let's start from the beginning. We know all three men are in the jewelry store. The cops arrive, boom, Darren Foster runs out the back exit and Paul Cooper runs out one of the side exits. If you're a scared 19 year old kid, do you follow your dad or someone you barely know?"

"His dad," James said.

"That's right," Henry said. "But, let's look past that. He's scared. Maybe, he panics and follows Paul Cooper. But he has a cop right on his tail. Officer Stewart said that Bobby was running behind the gunman. Bobby is 19, from his picture, he appeared to be in great physical shape. He should run right past an overweight, middle-aged Paul Cooper."

"But Bobby is in much better shape than his dad," James said. "Wouldn't he have run past him too?"

"No, for two reasons. Bobby trusted his father to lead him to safety, and second, I think Bobby cared enough about his father to stand in between him and a cop yelling for them to stop." Henry paused to scratch his head. "The facts just don't point toward Paul Cooper as the gunman."

"So, you think it's the father."

"Well, I think it is perfectly reasonable that Bobby followed his father out of that jewelry store, and chose to jog behind him as they tried to escape. I also believe that Bobby might have stopped and Darren kept running." Henry abruptly stopped talking and began to slowly shake his head again. "But, he wouldn't have shot his son."

"What? Why not?"

"Because he doesn't own a gun and because he can barely shoot one. Why would he, of all people, bring a gun to rob a closed jewelry store?"

"Maybe Paul brought an extra gun and gave it to Darren."

"Good thought," Henry said, nodding slightly. "But even if that was the case, Darren wouldn't have shot it."

"Don't be so sure," James said, wagging his finger. "Maybe, it happened like Paul Cooper said. He was aiming at the cop and shot his son by mistake. We know he was a lousy shot."

"Yes, we know that, but, more importantly, Darren knew that. He would never fire a gun anywhere near his son's direction."

"Wait a minute, what are you saying?" James said. "First, you say Paul didn't shoot Bobby. Now, you say Darren didn't either. You have eliminated both suspects."

Eric J. Lee

"That's right, I did." The two men just looked at each other in silence.

"Henry?" James slowly said. "Have you gone mad?"

"I hope not," Henry said with a smirk. "Here's what I think happened. Darren runs out the back exit and Paul runs out the side exit. I think Bobby tried to maximize his odds that the one cop entering the store did not follow him. So, he exited the *other* side exit. Unfortunately for Bobby, Officer Stewart chose to follow him. She yelled for him to stop and I'm guessing he didn't. I noticed the officer is very young. So, she likely has little experience. She panics and shoots a fleeing, unarmed man in the back."

"No, no, no," James said, grabbing a picture of the body. "Based on how they found the body, the shot had to come from the opposite end of the alley."

"James, come on. Officer Stewart moved the body to support her story."

"Moved the body? Not one of my officers. Nah, I don't think so."

"You never found the bullet, did you? The bullet that went through the victim. You haven't found it yet, right?"

James fell back in his chair, stunned. "How did you know?"

"Because your team is looking in the wrong area," Henry said. "They're looking in the south side of the alley because Officer Stewart said the gunman shot back toward her. But, if Officer Stewart shot the bullet, it would be somewhere on the north side of the alley, where I am guessing that forensics hasn't looked yet."

"I just can't believe this," James said, shaking his head. "She's a good officer."

"You have more evidence against her. You have the dying words of Bobby Foster."

156

"What are you talking about?" James asked. "All Bobby said was the word 'please'. That doesn't tie in Officer Stewart. Not in any way."

"Your officer on the phone said that Bobby was speaking softly, right?" James nodded. Henry said, "He misheard Bobby. When your officer asked who shot him, Bobby didn't say please, P-L-E-A-S-E. He said P-O-L-I-C-E. Please, police, when you're speaking softly, sound the same." James' eyes bulged out as the realization hit that one of his own was behind this. If it makes you more comfortable, wait to arrest Officer Stewart until you find that bullet on the north side of the alley and ballistics confirms it came from the same gun model and type as Officer Stewart's."

"Well, I must say that I'm impressed," James said. "You may be retired, but your mind never stopped working."

Shades of Gray

In every story, the author sets up two characters. The protagonist, an honorable person who can do no wrong and the villain, an evil character bent on destruction. But, that's not real life. In the real world, there are no pure heroes or pure villains. There are no absolutes: no black, no white. Instead, merely shades of gray.

The closest thing to a hero in my book is Rodney Mason. He doesn't save elderly women from burning buildings. But, every day he was kind and respectful to everyone whose path he crossed, regardless of class, race, or religious beliefs. Rodney was always impeccably neat and well groomed. Clean cut and straight as an arrow, twenty-five year old Rodney didn't do drugs, drink alcohol, or smoke cigarettes. Newly married with a child on the way, Rodney's life was going exactly according to plan. He prided himself on being responsible, always putting the welfare of his wife, and family first. Even his career came before personal pleasures. These are all good things.

But in life, you can have too much of a good thing. Take water, for example. You need water to survive. Without it, you'd dehydrate. But, if you were forced to consume over five gallons of water in one sitting, the sodium level in your body would drop, your brain would swell until you die. Imagine that: drinking water could kill you.

I wanted to bring out the spontaneity and the fun in Rodney's life. Just once, I wanted him to put himself first. I feared he'd wake up one day a sixty-year-old without any memorable, wildly fun experiences. I became acquainted with

Rodney for the first time at a work party. Over the next couple of months, about once a week, Rodney and I would go out on the town. He would let loose and, for that one night, forget any stresses in his life.

Once, we got home after one a.m. and Rodney's wife, Mary, was waiting for him in the living room. She glared at me and then said to him, "You're late. You should have called. I've been worried sick."

"Sorry," Rodney muttered, staggering toward the couch.

"Are you drunk?" she asked him.

Rodney looked at Mary with glazed eyes. "No," Rodney finally responded, as he sank into the couch.

Mary sighed heavily, before sitting down next to him on the couch. She said, "Look at me." When Rodney turned toward Mary, she put her hand on his knee. "You're going to be a dad soon. You have to be more responsible."

"I'm always responsible. Maybe, I'm sick of being responsible. Maybe, I'm sick of being perfect!" I sat on the coffee table, simply watching the confrontation. It was fascinating. Rodney buried his face in his hands and said, "I just can't take this anymore."

Then, the conversation switched to me. She accused Rodney of being under my influence, as if I were the reason he was speaking his mind so forcefully. That was just a cop-out. Yes, I may have encouraged him a little. But, there was nothing that Rodney did tonight that he did not want to do.

Mary leaned closer to Rodney, coming face-to-face with him. "I don't want you going out late at night without me anymore. Okay?"

"What am I? Your child now?!"

Mary grabbed Rodney by the chin, "Listen to me. You need to calm down."

Rodney, shocked by Mary's actions, acted instinctively. "Let go of me!" he shouted, before slapping Mary in the face.

Mary took a few steps back, rubbing her reddening face in shock. Rodney immediately fell to his knees, apologizing hysterically.

Time seemed to stop as the realization of what had happened set in for Mary. "You can sleep on the sofa tonight," she said, before racing upstairs.

The next day, it became apparent that I was not allowed to ever show up in Rodney's house again, wife's orders. Without his wife knowing, Rodney still sought me out. I am not sure if it was for old times sake or to get his mind off his problems. I started seeing him at lunch, something that never used to happen, and at least once a week after work.

One day, we had a long lunch at a local sports bar together. He became entranced with a NCAA basketball game on TV and lost track of the time. "Damn!" Rodney exclaimed, realizing he was going to be late for an important proposal meeting. He ran to the meeting three blocks away, but was too late.

Jane, Rodney's boss, greeted him in the lobby. "You're thirty-five minutes late. They cancelled our meeting and won't reschedule." Jane frowned at him. "What happened?"

"I just lost track of time," Rodney said, meekly.

"This is so unlike you. I don't know what your problem is lately," Jane said, shaking her head. "Just show me the marketing slides."

Rodney opened his briefcase and began frantically looking in it. "I must have left them at the bar."

"The bar?" Jane repeated. "Look, I suggest you go home and come back on Monday with a set of revised marketing slides for our next proposal, or your letter of resignation."

A lump formed in Rodney's throat as he watched her walk away. Then, he got a glimpse of himself in a nearby mirror. From the run over, his shirt was un-tucked, his tie crooked, and his hair a bit of a mess. He didn't recognize the man in the mirror. Why was his life, which normally went perfectly according to plan, falling apart?

He began to feel depressed, and as has been the case over the last month, he turned to me to get him through this. Instead of going home as Jane had instructed, he picked me up and drove to the top of a hill, which overlooked the city. We sat in the car for over an hour, listening to another NCAA basketball game on the radio. Every now and then, Rodney would mutter disparaging remarks about his boss and his job.

Like I said, every story has a hero and a villain. I suppose this is the point where the author identifies the villain. Obviously, Rodney is our hero. By now, I suppose the reader has pegged me as the villain. Before he met me, his life was perfect. And now, it appeared to be going downhill. I admit that I am not always the best influence on Rodney. But, it's a mistake to blame all of his problems on me.

Hear this. I am no villain. In fact, as Rodney sat in his car looking out at the city, I was helping him forget all his problems. I was making him feel better. One thing that Rodney knows: I am there for him, no matter what. And that's a good thing, right? He began to relax and his anger at Jane subsided. A smile actually returned to his face and he chuckled as he started the car. Things weren't that bad after all.

It was a three-minute drive to Rodney's house. When we arrived, he opened the garage door and pulled in. Not judging spacing effectively, he smashed into the back corner of Mary's car. Rodney eyes widened as he turned off the engine. How could he have hit the car?

"Oh my Gosh!" Mary said, racing from the house toward the driver's side of the car. "What happened? Are you…" Mary stopped in mid-sentence when she spotted me in the passenger's seat. "Oh Rodney," Mary said, with a look of disappointment. She immediately blamed me for the accident. Rodney came to my defense, but that only angered Mary more. Finally, she gave the ultimatum. It was either me or her. He couldn't have us both.

And that's the last I ever saw of Rodney. I really thought he would come back to me. I stood out on a billboard off a highway that he took every day on his way home. But, he purposely looked away. I often made my way back into his home, via the television, starring in several commercial ads. But, he would just change the channel. Rodney seemed to have more resolve than ever to stay away from me. Perhaps, it was the weekly meetings where he admitted he was addicted to me.

I still contend that I am no villain. I have a healthy relationship with millions of people. It's just that Rodney and I didn't mix well. Maybe I did damage his marriage, his job and his wife's car. Eventually, I probably would have hurt Rodney, maybe even killed him. As it relates to Rodney, I guess I was too much of a good thing. Remember, drinking too much water, let alone alcohol, can kill you.

The Job

People joke about it, but I don't think it's funny.
I'll do any job if I get paid enough money.

A million dollars is making me complete this assignment with
extra passion.
A million dollars has turned me into the world's most ruthless
assassin.

The intended victim is a Sarah, a mother of three.
The story is her rich husband wants her dead so he can be free.

Sometimes, I'm ashamed of the things that I agree to do,
And I know the effect it has on so many lives, children's too.

Some people have vilified my character and I have little to say
in defense.
My character has serious flaws and some actions simply don't
make sense.

I'm not asking for sympathy because the decision to take this job
was all mine.
"If I didn't take it, someone else would have," is my tired old
line.

I crouch down in the bushes waiting for my cue,
Trying not to think of the unspeakable violence I'm about to do.

Eric J. Lee

I spot my target, a woman approaching in the distance.
With her age and strength, no one would expect her to put up
much resistance.

With each step, she gets a little bigger in size,
But, with each step, she also gets closer to her demise.

The light skip in her step shows she didn't know danger is near,
Her happy whistle is a clue that she has no fear.

Once she passed me, I caught up to her to ask her the time.
She looked at her lighted watch and said that it was quarter to
nine.

"That's a good time to die," I said, thinking that was a corny
line.
I made a menacing sneer and readied myself to commit a
horrible crime.

"Don't move," I commanded, pulling my gun out.
Her jaw dropped immediately, too stunned to even shout.

The woman begged for her life and frantically offered her purse.
"I told you to be quiet!" I said angrily, before starting to curse.

To be in this business, you sometimes have to act callous and
mean.
I geared myself up for what was going to be a sick, gory scene.

I thought, "Understanding how someone could be so evil is hard
to figure,"
As I pointed the gun at her head and pulled the trigger.

The Job

Her body went limp and she fell to the ground,
She landed with a thud, a sickening sound.

I sighed at my contribution of another violent murder for the
whole world to see.
But the thought of even one copycat murder is what really
bothered me.

Getting typecast as the villain can put you in a rut,
But I maintain my menacing sneer toward the camera until the
director yells cut.

The Love Life of Louie Lancaster

Forty-year-old Louie Lancaster sat in his car in the parking lot outside of the classy La Finestra Italian restaurant. His hands shook with nervous anticipation. In his obsession to be on time, he had arrived thirty minutes early, thanks to unusually light traffic for a Friday evening. Louie grabbed the rear view mirror and angled it toward him. "Look at yourself, you're a wreck," he said, as drops of perspiration dribbled down his side of his face. "Relax, everything will be okay." Adrenaline pumped through his body as his head began to ache. He took a deep breath, laid his head back on the headrest, and thought back to the events that brought him to this parking lot.

Based on appearance, the handsome Louie was the personification of success: a beautiful wife, two well adjusted kids, a successful career as a building contractor, and a large estate in an upscale neighborhood. But sometimes appearances can be deceiving.

His twelve-year-long marriage was now an unmitigated disaster. The first nine years, however, were pretty darn good. He fell in love with a beautiful and bright real estate broker named Carla. The two became business partners, shortly before becoming partners in marriage. As pressures of the business and raising two kids mounted, Louie's and Carla's marriage suffered. They argued constantly. Before long, their love life became extinct and Louie moved into the guest bedroom permanently. They each considered divorce over the last two years, but in the interest of their young children, they decided to stay married. Their prenuptial agreement also gave a financial incentive to stay together. In the absence of physical abuse or adultery, the spouse who sought a divorce would only get 10% rather than half of their assets that they had accumulated during the marriage, which was over five million dollars.

In the last six months, Louie and Carla were husband and wife in name only. They were neither lovers nor friends. Their arguments were now so commonplace and vicious, the only way they could avoid them was to stop talking to each other. They behaved like a divorced couple, almost always doing things with the kids without the other. Using notes and voicemail whenever they had to communicate, they made it a priority to simply stay out of each other's way.

Louie fell into a deep depression, which bottomed out one Saturday night. He was having dinner with Kevin Salazar, his best friend who happened to also be his lawyer. They were sitting in the dining room of Kevin's bachelor pad eating take-out Chinese food. Kevin was doing all the talking while Louie stared vacantly at his chow mein. Finally, Louie spoke. "I'd really like some apple pie. Can you go out and get me some?"

"Sure," Kevin said, rising as he wiped his hands with a napkin. "There's a grocery store down the street. Let's go."

"No, I'll stay here."

"Oh," Kevin said, startled. "Okay, well make yourself at home. I'll be right back." As soon as Kevin left, Louie got up and walked into Kevin's closet in his bedroom. He knew right where Kevin kept his gun. He grabbed it off a shelf and checked the chamber. There was one bullet. A swarm of emotions ran through Louie's body and his mind raced. Thinking about his home life, he felt sad, frustrated, helpless, and ashamed. He just wanted to make the negative feelings go away. Standing in the middle of Kevin's bedroom, Louie's hands shook as he raised the gun to his head.

At that moment, the front door slammed shut. "I forgot my wallet!" Kevin exclaimed before stopping abruptly in the hallway in front of his bedroom. "Hey! Put the gun down!"

Louie began to tear up, adding embarrassment to his emotion of total despair. Louie threw the gun down on the bed and collapsed on the floor.

Two weeks and several therapy sessions later, Louie and Kevin met at a bar to have a few beers. Louie remembered the conversation as if it were yesterday.

"Louie, man, I'm worried about you," Kevin said. "All you do is work and sit at home. You haven't thought about, um, you know, suicide?"

"No," Louie said, shaking his head.

Kevin looked directly at Louie. "Your marriage, that's the root of your depression?"

Louie leaned forward with gritted teeth. "I loved my wife. I loved her with all my heart and soul. Then, all of a sudden, it was like she died." Louie looked down at his bottle of beer and shook his head. "No, it's actually worse than if she died, because I'm still forced to see her every day, constantly reminded of what seems so close and possible, but is really so far away and unattainable. Each day, I have to smell her scent-laided perfume and listen to her familiar voice, but I can't communicate with her. I have to look at her pretty face and beautiful body, but I can't touch her." Louie downed some alcohol before adding, "So, yeah, I'd say my marriage has a way of depressing me."

Kevin dropped his head slightly, at a loss for words. "I wish I could say something to salvage your marriage, but I can't. It's over and it's not coming back. I think it's time you start meeting other women."

"You know I can't take that risk. If I commit adultery, I'll lose..."

"I know, I know," Kevin said, waving his hand. "I'm the one who wrote your prenuptial agreement so I know what it says. But, mere dating is not adultery." Kevin paused to drink his beer before saying, "Come on, you know that Carla has been dating."

"I suspected as much," Louie said, gritting his teeth. "Still, if Carla finds out, she could try to make a case for..."

"She'd have no case." Kevin handed Louie a card. "I've been on this dating website and I met this real cool woman. She's not my type, but I think you two would hit it off. You should email her. And since you are so obsessed with your wife finding out, use a different name. Make up a different persona." Louie rubbed his face as he looked down at the card. Kevin took the card back and said, "Here, I'll write her email address down. Just mention that you're a friend of mine when you email her."

That night, Louie emailed the woman, whose name was Sandy. They hit it off immediately. He told Sandy that his name was Frank, a single dentist with no kids. Even though it was just through a computer, having a relationship with a woman changed his entire outlook on life. It was new and exciting. He looked forward to emailing her every day at work. There was no better feeling when a new message from Sandy arrived. He saved every email and often went back to re-read them. Each time he did, it lifted his spirits. Finally, after two months of exchanging emails, Louie got the nerve to ask whether Sandy would like to meet. She told him, "Yes."

Louie's excitement about the upcoming meeting was tempered by questions. What would Sandy think about *his* exaggerations, or outright lies? A single dentist with no kids? How could he tell her that he's married? Could he explain that, although he was married, he wasn't really in a marriage?

Despite the potential for rejection, Louie knew he had to meet her because it could be his only opportunity at happiness. He decided to keep the date a complete secret, even to his buddy Kevin. This morning, he left a note with Carla saying, "I'll be at the office late tonight. Your night to watch the kids." It was a message he had given her many times in the past, so he doubted that it would cause any suspicion.

Louie's headache began to subside as he rested in his car outside La Finestra Italian restaurant. He looked at his watch. It was 5:55 PM, five minutes before he was scheduled to meet Sandy for the first time. Louie left his car and walked into the restaurant. He approached the maitre d', who informed him that the other person in his party had not arrived, but offered to seat Louie at his reserved table.

"Sure," Louie said.

"Here you are sir," the maitre d' said, gesturing toward a booth. Louie decided to sit on the side that, although far away, had a clear view to the entrance of the restaurant. Alone at the table and eyes trained on the lobby, Louie asked himself, "What if that's Sandy?" every time a woman entered the restaurant. His stomach was consumed with butterflies.

Then, a figure walked in who immediately caught Louie's attention. A sharp chill shot up his spine. The last person in the world that he wanted to see had come into the restaurant. It was his wife, Carla.

Louie's heartbeat quickened and he immediately hid his face behind the menu. After a few moments, he peered above the menu and saw Carla walk in the opposite direction toward the restrooms. He breathed a sigh of relief. It appeared that Carla didn't see him.

"Hi, my name is Michael and I'll be your server," a waiter said, startling Louie. Embarrassed, Louie put the menu back on the table. "Anything to drink while you wait for your other party, sir?"

"No, no thank you. I'm fine." The waiter nodded and left. When Louie looked back over to the lobby, Kevin was approaching his table.

"Kevin! What are you doing here?"

"Just getting dinner," Kevin replied. "Hey, out on a Friday night. I love it. Are you with anyone?"

"She's not here yet," Louie said.

"She?" Kevin repeated, with a smile. "You dog. Who's the lucky lady?"

"Sandy," Louie said.

"You're kidding. The woman you've been emailing. You're meeting her in person?"

"Yeah, for the first time."

"I can't believe you didn't tell me. Well, that's great," Kevin said before sitting across from Louie. Kevin pointed to himself, saying, "And you have me to thank for that."

"There's just one problem," Louie said, glancing toward the waiting area. "Carla is here. I saw her walking toward the restroom."

"Carla?" Kevin said, looking back over his shoulder toward the lobby. "Are you sure?"

"Yes. Look, I'm going to need you to run interference. You can't let her see me."

"I think you're being paranoid. Having dinner with a woman is not an affair, legally or morally."

He looked directly at Kevin. "I need this favor. Go to the waiting area and make sure she doesn't come anywhere near this table." Kevin paused for a moment as if he was weighing whether he wanted to get involved. "Can you do this?"

"Sure," Kevin finally said. He was about to get up when a woman arrived at their table.

"Kevin!" a voice boomed. Both men looked up. It was Carla. She looked directly at Kevin, not acknowledging Louie's presence. "Come on, we have to go."

"We? You guys are here together?" Louie said.

"Relax," Kevin said. "We're just having dinner."

"Kevin," Carla said, becoming more agitated. "Let's go."

Louie glared at Kevin, realizing he had been betrayed. "Hold on," he said to Kevin. Louie turned and said to Carla, "Sit down." When she didn't move, Louie added as he dipped his head, "Please?"

Carla sighed before sitting next to Kevin. "You have two minutes," Carla said, looking at her watch. "What do you want?"

"What are you doing here with Kevin?" Louie asked. "You said you were going to be home with the kids."

Carla leaned forward. "You know what they say about people in glass houses. This doesn't look like your office. So, I guess we're even." Carla looked at her watch again. "You've got a minute and forty seconds."

Louie shook his head and squinted his eyes. "You didn't answer my question. "What are you doing here with Kevin?"

Carla paused to quickly look at Kevin before saying, "I've met another guy and he's wonderful. He's everything that you're not: kind, caring, funny. The best thing about him is that he makes me feel good about myself. You haven't done that for me in years."

Louie fumed inside, as it was clear that Carla's words were meant to hurt him. "You're dating Kevin now. Is that it?"

"As usual, you're clueless," Carla said, happy she had gotten under Louie's skin. "And don't get on your high horse. Kevin told me you've been dating too."

"You told her about Sandy?" Louie said, shooting Kevin a piercing glare.

Carla's smile disappeared. "Kevin! Tell me you didn't."

Eric J. Lee

"I did," Kevin said.

"What's going on?" Louie asked.

Kevin paused a moment before saying, "Allow me to introduce you two, since you haven't met in person." Kevin gestured with his hand as he said, "Sandy, this is Frank. Frank, Sandy."

Louie's jaw dropped. "She's the woman I connected with over the past two months?" Kevin answered with a slow nod. "Why did you do this?"

"Yeah, and how could you lie to us?" Carla asked Kevin.

"You both were miserable," Kevin said. "Louie even tried to commit suicide. Look, I thought if I could give you two a new beginning, your marriage might work." Louie and Carla looked at each other, still stunned. "And I didn't lie. I told both of you I wanted to introduce you to a friend of mine. Both of you are friends of mine. And that's why I did it. You two are friends of mine."

"I can't believe that you're Sandy," Louie said, shaking his head as he stared at Carla.

"Now, I need you two to do me a favor," Kevin said. "I want you to have dinner, at least for this one night, as Frank and Sandy, not Louie and Carla." The couple nodded slightly, which was Kevin's cue that it was time to leave.

The Stranger

I yawned as I fastened my checkered robe and headed downstairs, looking forward to my morning coffee. I stopped suddenly as I reached the bottom of the stairs when I saw a stranger in my living room.

"Whoah! Who are you?"

The old man, who was sitting on the sofa reading a magazine, slowly stood up. "I'm Pete. I live just down the street."

"Um… you mind explaining how you got in my house?"

"Oh, your wife Sara let me in."

"Where is she?" I asked.

"She just left to pick up some eggs at the market. She'll be back in a minute." I walked over to Pete, who had a white mustache and beard. He looked at me and snickered, "Nice robe."

"Hey," I said, wagging my finger at him. "I'm a married man with both kids away at college. I come downstairs expecting my wife. You're lucky I have any clothes on at all."

Pete laughed. "I saw your wife outside and she invited me over for breakfast. I'm new in the neighborhood and I like to know my neighbors." Pete paused for a moment. "I have a question I like to ask to get to know people better. It's a little strange though. Do you mind?"

I sat down in a chair near Pete. "Go right ahead."

"If you could have breakfast with four people in the world from any time in history, who would they be?"

"Ooh… that's a good one," I said, looking at the ceiling to think. "Well, my dad for sure. He died three years ago. Jackie Robinson. I'm a huge baseball fan. Lucille Ball. She'd keep the conversation light."

"That's sounds like a great group," Pete said with a smile. "You have one more."

"My wife Sara, no question."

"What? You can have breakfast with your wife anytime. This is a special, once in a lifetime breakfast."

I shook my head. "Sara is the love of my life. She's the one that would make the breakfast special."

Pete frowned and he paused to think. "Let's say you couldn't invite her."

"Then I would just have those three," I said, tiring of the question. I got up and walked over to the window. It was a beautiful, sunny day. "How long ago did Sara leave for the market?" There was no response. I turned around to look at Pete. "Did you hear me?"

"I did," Pete said, scratching his head. I must confess I haven't been completely honest with you. You won't be seeing Sara. Not for a very long time."

"What?" I said as my heart started to race. "What have you done with her?"

"I promise you that she is fine."

I rushed over to the sofa and leaped on top of the old man. I pressed my forearm up against his neck. I was much stronger than him. "Game time is over. You tell me where my wife is and you tell me now!"

"Okay, I will tell you everything, but please get off me," Pete said, straining to speak.

I released the pressure I was putting on Pete's neck, but I still had him pinned on the sofa. "I'm not letting you go until you tell me what is going on."

"I know this is tough for you. That's why I arranged a little surprise in the dining room. Breakfast is ready."

"I don't care about breakfast. Where's my wife?" I said, exerting pressure again, but this time on his shoulder.

"You don't understand. Your dream breakfast guests are all here. Your dad, Jackie Robinson, and Lucille Ball."

I released the pressure on his shoulder and stared at Pete for a moment. "Did you escape from some insane asylum?"

"I'm serious. I have arranged it all. They're in your dining room right now. Go look."

I glared at Pete, figuring this was some kind of trick. I grabbed him by the arm and forcefully led him down the hallway toward the dining room. As we approached the dining room, I stopped suddenly. My heartbeat quickened and my eyes widened. I heard Lucille Ball's distinctive voice. She said something which triggered my Dad's signature laugh. A laugh I have not heard in three years. My dad was alive!

I released my hold on Pete and stared at him. "You can bring people back from the dead?"

"No," Pete said, shaking his head. "No one has the power to do that."

"But… then how?"

Pete smiled and said, "Welcome to heaven."

Crime Time

"Crime in our town has gone up for the seventh straight month. Police are at a loss for the reason. They are warning all citizens to be on their guard."

"Hopefully, not too much on their guard," Spencer said with a chuckle. He turned off the radio as he sat in his pickup truck. His eyes were trained on the liquor store as he watched the only remaining customer leave.

"It's show time," Spencer said to himself as he put on a black ski mask. As he walked across the empty parking lot toward the store, the young man felt powerful, in complete control of his destiny.

As Spencer entered the store, he spotted the cashier behind the counter, looking down at a magazine. "Get your hands up!" Spencer shouted, pointing a gun at the cashier, Tom.

Tom's eyes bulged out as he raised his shaking arms in the air. "Please, don't shoot."

"You do what I say and I won't. Keep your hands where I can see them at all times. Go over to the front door and lock it."

With perspiration dripping down his face, Tom slowly walked over to the front door and locked it. At Spencer's order, Tom drew the blinds on the large window so no one could see inside and then he flipped the small sign around to show "closed."

"Okay, back to the cash register," Spencer said, gesturing with his gun. "Hey, old man," Spencer said as Tom walked back behind the counter. "Don't be a hero and try anything, alright." He tossed him a bag. "Open the register and fill it."

Tom worked quickly, stuffing all of the bills in the bag. As soon as he was done, he lifted his hands back in the air.

"The bills under the tray too," Spencer said, dipping his head. As Tom lifted the tray to reveal larger bills, Spencer glanced at his stop watch. The plan was for the whole job to take less than five minutes. It had been a minute and thirty five seconds. "You're doing a great job, old man."

"I've had practice. This is the third time this year we've been robbed."

"You own this place?" Spencer asked. Tom shook his head. "Then what are you whining about?"

Tom wanted to tell the gunman about the nightmares he has had since the last hold up. He wanted to tell him, due to the recent crime spree, how he did not feel safe anymore. But most of all, he wanted to tell him how his heart beat so quickly he worried he was about to have a heart attack. But, he tempered these thoughts, remained quiet, and stuffed the last bill in the bag.

"Good, but that's not all of it. Take me to the safe." Tom hesitated. "Now!" Spencer shouted.

Tom led him to the back of the store. He unlocked the door which revealed a safe and began to work the combination. Within a minute, he had opened the safe and began dumping the cash contents into Spencer's bag.

"So, all told, how much you think we got in the bag?" Spencer asked.

Tom put the last stack of bills in the bag before pausing to think. "That's got to be over three grand."

Spencer looked at his stop watch and smiled. "Not bad for three minutes and fifty seconds of work." The $3,000 pay day may seem small, but he needed that money badly. Spencer grabbed the bag full of money and instructed Tom to lie face down on the floor and count to a thousand. "If you want to stay alive, don't get up until you reach a thousand." With that, Spencer closed the door and headed out.

As the door closed, Tom's body relaxed. The door locked automatically when it closed, so he was safe. An overwhelming sense of relief came at the realization that he survived another armed robbery. He felt proud about how coolly he handled himself, although bitter to be put in that position again. He wondered whether the young gunman would ever understand what he put his victims through.

Spencer raced out the front door of the store. Luckily, there was no one around to even try to stop him. The parking lot was completely empty. "Wait a minute," Spencer thought. "The parking lot is too empty." He stopped and his jaw dropped. He clutched his chest, feeling his rapidly beating heart. "No!" he shouted in disbelief. His $15,000 truck…. stolen.

Bad Morning

I woke up in an unfamiliar room with a terrible pain in my stomach. I could hear people in the next room and screamed to get their attention.

Finally, the tall woman came into the room. She began speaking a language I didn't understand. I cried loudly to show her I was in pain. Not comprehending, she offered me a drink.

I pushed the drink away and screamed at her to do something. She just stood there, looking at me.

I tried to tell her that my stomach hurt, but I don't think she understood. She gave me a hug, patting my back. "Why did she do that?" I thought before burping. Surprisingly, I felt better and stopped screaming. Then, she put me back in my crib.

About the Stories

WARNING: This section should not be read until AFTER you have read all of the stories in this book. In this section, I do give away some of the clues, climax, and conclusion of the stories.

Sometimes, as a mystery writer I feel like I am playing a shell game. Through misdirection and fancy moves, I challenge the reader to find the murderer. Is the murderer under shell number 1, 2 or 3? I believe the best mystery stories challenge the reader to think outside the box, or shell, so to speak.

I don't like stories that are formulaic and trite. The perfect story would have the reader guess the wrong shell three times, only to see it sitting on the corner of the table in plain view the whole time.

As much as I like the image of the shell game, a mystery story must be much more than that. It must capture the reader's imagination with its plot and their heart with its characters. I believe the most important part of a mystery story is the ending. Does it make sense? Was it satisfying? Still, even the most powerful ending in the world will be useless if the reader is not drawn in to finish the story.

So, I guess I liken myself to an airline pilot. In order to have happy customers, they better like their destination. But, equally important, they better enjoy the trip along the way.

Eric J. Lee

Murder in a Coastal Town

I worked hard to make the title story pack an emotional wallop. I wanted the reader to feel for each character. The narrator had a different viewpoint than his brother or his wife. Who was right and who was wrong? Could it be both parties were right? That was the issue I wanted to explore. In life, when should we focus on justice or even revenge versus "turning the page" to look toward the future?

Some people who have read a lot of my stories have come to expect a twist. For those readers, I tried to set a trap in this story. I wanted the reader to think that it might be the brother since Ashley actually says that it was a man wearing a hooded shirt and then says it was her dad. Wearing a hood, her uncle would look like her dad. This clearly would be red herring because the brother would have no logical motive for killing Tyler. Mercy killing or aversion to paying a loan would fall way short of a motive. From early reviews, not too many veteran readers fell for this trap.

I wrote this story trying to be true to the fact that a frustrated Ashley simply pushed Tyler. However, she did not intend to push him off the cliff. She just wanted to push him away. She obviously feels a tremendous amount of guilt. She doesn't even want to be near the cliff again. Her response when her father pressed her for details about Tyler's death, is telling. She simply said, "Tyler fell", not that some "stranger pushed him." When she was pressed further, she simply said, "Someone pushed him". Only after a long pause and a lot of pressing, she fell back to her original story that it was a hooded man. Then, when her mom was approaching, in order to end the conversation, she erratically says it was her dad. Clearly, Ashley is not a good liar, nor a mastermind murderer, just a frightened, guilt-ridden kid.

Murder at Buckley Liquors

I am a fan of courtroom dramas, so I leaped at the challenge of writing a story around a murder case. This plot took off and became, by far, the longest story that I have ever written. Despite the length of the story, I tried to keep the same discipline that I employ with short stories. My re-writing process was ruthless, cutting out everything I felt wasn't absolutely necessary to keep the plot moving and the story tight.

The trial section was challenging to write because, for the most part, the narrator is passively watching the case. I had to keep the readers interest and suspense even though there was little action other than witness testimony. I re-wrote the opening of the story several times, opting to go with the most attention-grabbing version. I cut out the background of receiving the juror summons and waiting for a case and went straight to the narrator being in the jury box. Opening arguments in the case actually begin on the top of page 2 in order to get right into the witness testimony.

The jury deliberation section was fun to write. I have served on a jury twice in my life and used a lot of my experiences to write this section. I wanted the frustration that these jurors feel to mirror the emotions in the jury I served. Some readers felt that the jury deliberations went a little too long, but I wanted the reader, without becoming bored, to feel a little of the fatigue that the characters in the story felt. Getting twelve Americans with varying ages, education, race, and life experiences to all agree can be a real challenge. As frustrating an experience being a juror can be, I think every American should experience it. It will shed a different light on our justice system.

I have come to the conclusion that the selection of the jury is the most critical part of any case. Making sure you can get a group of people who are more acceptable to hearing your side of the story in your way is the key to winning the case. I assembled three mock juries to read the first part of "Murder at Buckley Liquors". One came to a consensus of not guilty, one was hung, but overwhelming guilty, and one was hung with an even deadlock between guilty and not guilty. The three mock juries had the same facts, but came to three dramatically different conclusions.

How effective can juror consultants be? How can anyone predict how someone will feel based on background information off a questionnaire. Before my mock juries convened, I took a shot at trying to predict how people would vote by the end of deliberations. Now, I know I have no special training in being a juror consultant. But, I knew the facts of the case better than anyone and I personally knew the members of the jury. Not from a basic questionnaire, but from years of friendship. Guess how I did at predicting whether they would end up voting guilty or not guilty? Not much better than 50% accuracy, which showed I am as about as accurate as flipping a coin.

The key fact that would have swayed me is Paul's decision to gas up when he would have had greater than a half a tank of gas. On a cold night with your wife waiting for romance, it just doesn't make sense to me. I was surprised how many people in my juries felt that this was not necessarily an important point.

More than any story I have ever written, there's a parade of characters, both in the jury box and on the witness stand. As far as witnesses, I wanted to build unique characters that the reader could have some emotional reaction (whether it be pity, sympathy, respect, or distrust). In the first draft of this story, I had Brad, who was the less trustworthy of the boys, be the one who witnessed Paul putting on his mask. But, I changed it to Alan, believing that it made Alan's testimony more believable (because he likely wouldn't lie) and Brad's more believable too (because he didn't lie about seeing him).

The Return of Henry Burrows

Sometimes, the best way to bake a casserole is to throw all of your favorite things in there and expect it to taste great. That was the plan with this story. There were a lot of things I wanted to do in an upcoming story and I decided to throw most of those things in this one. I wanted to write a story where it appeared like the murder was either person A or person B, due to the testimony of a trusted witness. I wanted to the reader to have tunnel vision that these were the only options. And lo and behold, it is not the suspect, but the witness.

I also had the idea of wanting a dying witness to whisper the identity of his killer. However, the message needed to initially be misunderstood. In this story, when asked who shot him, Bobby Foster mumbles "police", but the officer hears "please". This took me a long time to be happy with the misunderstood word. I must have gone through a hundred different options. However, once I stumbled across "police", I felt I had a winner.

My last idea to throw in this story was to bring back the character of Henry Burrows. Henry, who was lead character in *The Intuition of Henry Burrows*, is a favorite of mine. In a short story that had to move fast, I needed Henry's quick reasoning skills to pull off this story. I wanted an outsider from the police, who would be more open to suspecting Officer Stewart. However, I needed an insider, as well, who had access to all police records and investigations. As a well respected retired inspector, Henry was a perfect fit for this story.

Eric J. Lee

Shades of Gray

Have you ever looked at that famous drawing of a woman?
Most people look at the drawing and see a young woman, but if
you stare at it long enough, eventually you will see an elderly
woman. Like with the picture, sometimes in life, you will see
more things if you just take a moment to look at it in a different
way.

That's really what this story was all about. The reader
comes in with the expectation that the narrator is a human being,
perhaps a buddy. But, it turns out that the story is being told
from the perspective of a bottle of alcohol. Admittedly, this is a
strange premise. So, to be fair, I wanted to shape the framework
of this world very early in the story. In the very first page of the
story, I spent an entire paragraph discussing how water "could
kill you".

Then, throughout the story, I tried to stay true to the fact that
the narrator was a bottle of alcohol. During an argument
between Rodney and his wife, I wrote that "I sat on the coffee
table", which would be unusual for a human being. Rodney's
wife accused me of "being under my influence", parroting the
very common phrase of being under the influence of alcohol.
And in the story, after Rodney parties with me, his reactions are
over the top (unusual outbursts) and reckless (car accident in his
garage). His wife even accuses him of being drunk on the
second page. Even though he denies it, the description of his
"glazed eyes" and "staggering toward the couch" seems to
indicate otherwise.

Although I like telling this story through the eyes of the
alcohol, I think the story would have worked without this
perspective. At its core, it is a story about a man, who is
impeccably neat and extremely organized. He has a wonderful
marriage and a baby on the way. Then, his world falls apart. He
is late for a big meeting. He doesn't recognize the untidy and

tardy man in the mirror and his marriage is falling apart. He asks himself, "Why is my life which normally goes perfectly according to plan, falling apart?" and "How could I have hit the car?" Both questions clearly point to our narrator and unofficial "villain", alcohol.

The Job

I believe a story should stay true to its characters. Within the first eight sentences, the narrator admits that he is the "world's most ruthless assassin". I think the reader is left to hope that somehow, someway the woman may be spared her life. After a self-proclamation of the "world's most ruthless assassin", I wanted to stay true to the fact that nothing would deter his character from committing this murder.

Now, everyone understands the twist is that the narrator is an assassin in a movie, not in real life. When I wrote the first draft of this story, I thought I went overboard on the clues. I did think I could get away with using phrases like "the story is" and "my character has serious flaws". However, I thought saying "that was a corny line", "waiting for my cue", "have to act callous", and "a sick, gory scene" would be too much. The truth is a smaller percentage of people figure out this story than hardly any of other story that I've written. I believe that I was able to effectively space these clues. Another reason I think this story works is the title. From the very beginning, it helps sell "The Job" in the story as the hit man.

This is the third rhyming, mystery poem (one in each of my three books) that I have written. Great care has to be given to each line. Since the story is so few words, each sentence must be essential. To be effective, the rhyming should not be distracting or feel forced. I believe the poem would work without the rhyming at all. The plot and climax must stand on its own. However, the rhyme should be an added bonus, providing the poem pace and rhythm.

The Lovelife of Louie Lancaster

I held up the publishing of this book for two months because I simply wasn't happy with the climax of an earlier version of this story. The original version had a drawn out argument between Louie and Kevin, where Louie suspects Kevin of dating Carla. I believe this final version works better because the conflict is centered around Louie and Carla rather than Louie and Kevin.

This story was really about the connection of these former lovers. Whatever sparked their initial love was still there. There was so much despair in the Lancaster house that the couple just simply didn't know how to start to repair their marriage. They had stopped talking. They had stopped listening. In all respects, they had stopped caring. But, under aliases in email, they are able to find that special "something" that sparks the relationship. That special "something", which appeared lost forever, was still there.

In life, I have found when two people are in an intense, deeply rooted feud, the hardest part of ending the feud is the first steps. Neither party wants to be the one that "gives in". Both parties would rather be unhappy than lose face. This is what Kevin saw. As a good friend to both Louie and Sandy, he took the first step that both parties were unable to take. And in the process, he proved that the couple was still in love.

Some readers may wonder why Louie or Carla didn't walk out, once they realized what Kevin had done. After all, the couple had spent the last six months despising each other. I think they stayed for two reasons. First, they realized they had connected over email. And second, they liked and respected their friend Kevin and what he did for them.

The Stranger

This story played with the concept of perspective. The narrator is separated from the love of his life, his wife Sara. He is adamant in his belief that something happened to her. Instead, something has happened to him.

Throughout the story the narrator struggles with this concept. Even when he hears his father's laugh, he believes that his father was brought back from the dead as opposed to thinking something happened to him.

The title gives away the fact that this story has a lot to do with the identity of the stranger. I gave him the name "Pete", short for Saint Peter, the man meets you at the pearly gates. I described the stranger consistent with the image of Saint Peter.

Crime Time

The biggest clue in this story came in the very first sentence when the radio warns everybody to be on their guard against crime, and that includes Spencer.

This is a simple story of karma as Spencer realizes the same emotions as he had put his victims through. This story's word count at 752 is almost identical to *The Stranger*. Both stories deal with a simple concept and only a few characters.

I originally idea of this story was to convey the heartbreak and feelings of violation that crime victims feel. I should know. I have had my car stolen. I decided to proceed with the story when I felt I could have the twist of the criminal getting a taste of his own medicine.

Eric J. Lee

Bad Morning

One day, I was playing with a friend's baby and thought, "What must the world be like from his perspective?" This gave "birth" to the idea of this story. As I wrote that story, every word was meant to stay true to that reality. As an example, the baby says "the tall woman came into the room." The use of the word "the" indicates that this is how the baby specifically refers to this person he has seen many times before.

At 128 words, this is the shortest story that I have ever published. It was a true challenge to tell a satisfying story with so few words. I scrutinized every single word in this story.

One of the reasons that I like this story is that the reveal that the narrator is a baby (for most people) does not happen until the very last word.

Other short story collections by this author:

This book features ten short mystery and suspense stories sure to entertain, surprise, and intrigue the reader. In the short story, *Murder in a Country Town*, the narrator, an avid hunter, is obsessed with killing the sheriff of a small country town. What is at the root of the narrator's hatred? In a high stakes game of cat and mouse, exactly who has the upper hand? Will the narrator be successful, or will the hunter become the hunted?

In another story, a young accountant is working late in the office on a Friday night. Living alone, he calls home to leave himself a simple reminder message. Instead of hearing his answering machine, someone answers the phone. When he asks to speak to himself, the familiar voice says, "Speaking." He quickly comes to a startling realization. The voice sounds identical to his.

For more information about the author and his stories, please visit his official website at www.ericleestories.com

Other short story collections by this author:

This book features nine short mystery and suspense stories. In the short story, *Murder in a Coastal Town*, a homicide detective, is overcome with grief at the murder of his eight-year-old son. The only witness to the murder is his eleven-year-old daughter. How does he extract detailed information about the murder from a witness who is desperately trying to forget? Will the detective ever be able to catch the murderer and what emotional price is he willing to pay?

In another story, four guests arrive separately to a gated mansion. They realize they all played a central role in the conviction of Carols Rivera ten years earlier. They soon meet their host for the evening: recent prison escapee, Carols Rivera.

For more information about the author and his stories, please visit his official website at www.ericleestories.com

Other novels by this author:

Trying to Win at Love tells the funny and inspiring story of a new tennis captain pressed into running a local team because "there's no one else." As his own expectations for success rise, the rookie captain begins to equate wins as validation from his players and competitors. His troubles, which aren't limited to the court, soon mount as quickly as his victories. A group of colorful characters and extraordinary events teach him valuable lessons about winning on the court and in life.

For more information about the author and his stories, please visit his official website at www.ericleestories.com.

Other novels by this author:

In this humorous and inspirational sequel to the novel *Trying to Win at Love*, the narrator copes with several stinging losses. Faced with new challenges, he discovers that old approaches don't always provide the solution. Without the comfort and familiarity of the past, he struggles in his attempt to find a new team and mend a broken heart. In the process, he learns a lot about himself and life as he once again tries to win at love.

For more information about the author and his stories, please visit his official website at www.ericleestories.com. at www.ericleestories.com.